The
BRICK
HOUSE
Cafe

The
BRICK
HOUSE
Cafe

CARLA LAUREANO

LAUREANO
CREATIVE MEDIA

Published by Laureano Creative Media LLC
P.O. Box 460241
Aurora, CO 80046, U.S.A.
laureanocreativemedia.com

Cover design by Hillary Manton Lodge
Author photo by Reynaldo Laureano, copyright © 2023
Edited by Jocelyn Bailey
Copyedited by Denise Harmer

ISBN 978-1-960079-01-5 (sc)
ISBN 978-1-960079-00-8 (e-book)

ACKNOWLEDGMENTS

For something that is supposed to be such a solitary process, writing a book requires an awfully big cast of characters!

Big thanks to all the lovely people who contributed to the creation of this book: my fearless beta readers Meaghan Ahlbrand, Leslie Florea, and Deanne Patterson, whose honest feedback was invaluable to the shaping of the early drafts; my editor, Jocelyn Bailey, for her astute comments and sharp eye—I've wanted to work with you for ages, so I'm happy to finally have my chance; my copyeditor, Denise Harmer, for her attention to detail and dedication to making me look far more grammatically correct and punctuation-savvy than I actually am; my brilliant cover designer, Hillary Manton Lodge, whose vision and Photoshop magic constantly astounds me–this series is in such good hands; my good friends Amber Lynn Perry, Jen Turano, Lori Twichell, and Courtney Walsh—your support and belief makes me feel like I can accomplish anything! And last, my appreciation to you, dear reader, for continuing to support me by buying, requesting, sharing, and checking out my books. As much as I love writing for its own sake, it's not complete until it's in your hands. Thank you, thank you!

CHAPTER ONE

FOUR HOURS AFTER SHE'D LEFT DENVER, Mallory Adams had to admit that she was lost.

Well, not *lost*, exactly, or at least *she* wasn't. Her GPS was another story. It had acted all confident when it mapped her route from her motel just east of Denver to the southern, mountainous town of Salida, the town on which she was supposed to be writing an article for *Altitude Magazine*. Except now, instead of directing her to the mountain biking summer mecca, the app was having a nervous breakdown.

"Make a U-turn at the next light in 0.2 miles," it pronounced calmly in its cultured female AI voice.

Mallory squinted through the windshield, the bright light from the setting sun momentarily blinding her and leaving bright spots across her vision. "What light?" she muttered to herself. Right now, the road was simply a faded black ribbon marked by a dashed yellow line, stretching endlessly in a high plains landscape of scrub pine and piñon and ... dirt. She'd barely seen another car on the road—at six p.m. on a Friday night!—let alone enough traffic to actually necessitate a stoplight.

"Make a U-turn in one hundred yards," the map told her, completely unaware of Mallory's growing feeling that she was in the middle of an old *Twilight Zone* episode.

Almost too late, she saw the dusty road that intersected the highway, flipped on her blinker, and slowed. If it wanted her to make a U-turn, she would make a U-turn.

"Okay," she said aloud, "what now? Where do I go from here? Pretty sure coming back the way I came isn't going to help matters."

And now she was having a conversation with an app which was—hopefully—not sentient and completely unable to talk back. But what other choice did she have? She'd been going in circles ever since she started the slow climb into the mountains, watching the time to destination count down to zero and reset. She hadn't seen any gas stations, her cell service was spotty, and she really needed to get to Salida.

She never should have pitched this article to *Altitude*. She wasn't even really a writer. She'd done a lot of writing in her history grad program before she made the ill-fated decision to quit school, which had eventually led her to driving aimlessly across Colorado highways with everything she owned in the back of her Honda SUV. It was simply that her specialization on the nineteenth-century American West and the few articles she'd written about Idaho for local magazines had made her think that maybe she could actually make a go of it.

Or maybe it had just seemed like the only option after she broke up with her boyfriend and he kicked her out of the apartment they had shared.

It had been either that or haunt the same favorite spots in Boise, feeling pathetic while she looked for a place in a housing market that was nearly as aggressive and overpriced as Los Angeles or Denver, just waiting to run into John and the new girlfriend.

Though she couldn't say how new she was. Mallory had the vague idea this had been going on for some time, but to dwell too deeply on that thought would be to second-guess every evening he'd been gone and every time he'd said he had to work late. It would mean admitting to college friends that they had been right when they told her moving in with a guy she'd known for six months was a bad idea—as if relocating from Washington to Idaho for him wasn't a big enough show of stupidity. She never would have even considered it had she not rolled up her life in Seattle before she realized that she absolutely could not afford her own place in Boise.

So maybe driving aimlessly across the high plains of southern Colorado, looking for a destination that always seemed out of reach, was supposed to be a metaphor for the unanchored disaster her personal life had become.

"Turn left at the next intersection," the map proclaimed triumphantly, as if it had finally figured out where it was going.

"Okay, turning left at the next intersection," she said, flicking on the turn signal. There must be a town ahead, and she didn't even care if it was Salida. Given the coffee, the Big Gulp of Coke, and the half bottle of water she'd consumed while driving through the back roads of Colorado, finding a rest stop was becoming more important than finding her destination.

A few minutes later, the GPS dumped her out on what looked like a main street of a town. Slowly, she navigated her way down the near-empty thoroughfare, her hopes sinking with every building she passed. They weren't derelict, exactly. While some doors and windows were boarded up with plywood, the buildings themselves looked like they were in pretty good condition: lovely reddish-orange brick structures with white plasterwork around the windows and what looked like the original century-old glass, standing shoulder to shoulder with painted brick and the occasional timber facing. Their differing heights and crenellated tops had probably once given the street a whimsical air.

No, it felt more like the town had been holding its breath so long that when it finally exhaled, it had just given up, slumping in defeat. Kind of like a dog sent to the pound, finally resigning itself to its sad fate, accepting the unlikelihood of ever seeing its owners again.

The image hit Mallory soundly in the chest, but whether it was the defeated air of the town or the idea of a sad puppy—she never could abide the idea of animals in trouble—she didn't know. It didn't matter that it was completely fanciful, and as a mostly-trained historian, she dealt in facts, evidence, and the occasional well-educated conjecture. She couldn't shake the idea that this town was pining, and even more unsettling, that it had been waiting for her.

"You have reached your destination," the GPS voice announced proudly, and Mallory punched the *exit navigation* button harder than necessary. This was most certainly *not* Salida. It might not even be a bathroom break from the look of things. But the fact that there were cars parked along the street said there were people somewhere, and surely real live humans would be more accurate in getting her to her destination than this stupid malfunctioning phone app.

She noted one cluster of cars in front of a wide, three-story brick building on the corner up ahead. With a sigh of relief, she pulled into an empty parking space between a dusty black pick-up truck and a shiny Toyota SUV. Unlike the other buildings on the street, the plate glass windows here were clean, the door was painted in a fresh white that matched the window trim on the upper stories, and it had a cheery sign proclaiming it *The Brick House Cafe.* All these things added up to signs of life, but more importantly, signs of a proper restroom with running water.

"I apologize for every mean thing I ever said to you," she muttered to her phone. She grabbed her tote bag off the seat beside her and climbed out of the vehicle. For a second, Mallory pushed at her hair, her makeshift bun now listing at an alarming angle on the top of her head. She tried to pat it into place before she gave up. Why did she care anyway? She was officially in Nowhereville, USA. Who did she think she had to impress?

That question was answered for her in abundance when she pushed open the door to the cafe and found herself face-to-face with one of the more handsome men she'd come across in recent memory—tall and tan, with dark hair and dark eyes and a beard that hovered just on the right side of the dividing line between manicured and scruffy. Except while she was frozen in both appreciation and horror, he barely gave her a glance, instead more focused on the three plates he was balancing on both hands and one forearm.

"Be right with you," he muttered gruffly, before whisking the plates off to their rightful owners.

Heat flooded Mallory's face, but whether it was from embarrassment or the sudden, inexplicable thrill of attraction, she couldn't say. She yanked the scrunchy out of her bun and ran her fingers self-consciously through her hair a couple of times, trying to recall whether or not she'd bothered to put on makeup this morning before leaving her motel. She'd just settled on the unfortunate answer of *not* when the man came back, a slight smile on his lips. He pulled a menu from a basket near the register and gestured to the restaurant. "Booth or counter?"

She was set to say booth, but what came out when she opened her mouth was, "Counter."

"Sit where you'd like," he said indifferently and moved behind the counter again. When she picked a stool about halfway down, he placed the menu in front of her and pulled an ordering pad from his apron pocket. "Something to drink?"

"Coffee, please, black," she said, and found herself looking at the menu before she remembered why she was here. "Actually, can I use your restroom?"

"Back and to the left." He replaced the pad in his pocket. "I'll get your coffee."

Mallory smiled her thanks and then hightailed it through the restaurant in the direction he'd indicated. Only three tables were occupied, two of them by older couples who watched her curiously as she passed, the other by a teenager with a laptop, earbuds, and what looked like a biology textbook who did not mark her passing at all. She went straight to a stall, and when she emerged to her own reflection, she almost groaned aloud. It was worse than she'd thought. Not only had she *not* put on makeup this morning, she hadn't fully removed last night's mascara, which was now beneath her eyes in a look that was somewhere between smoky eye and raccoon.

"Figures," she muttered. "First good-looking guy I've come across in weeks and I look like this." She washed her hands, and after she dried them, used the damp paper towel to try to remove some of the makeup with only middling results. It was waterproof, and she wasn't about to use the industrial-strength soap in the pump at the sink. This would have to be good enough, especially considering he'd looked at her with as much interest as he might regard a fence post. It wasn't as if she was ever going to see him again anyway. She would get dinner, then ask for directions to Salida and be on her way to the B&B she'd booked just outside of town. The stupid-handsome stranger would just have to deal with her accidental haute couture makeup for the next forty-five minutes. Still, she gave her hair one last fluff, appreciating that the bun had given the usual stick-straight strands a slight wave before she turned out of the bathroom.

A steaming cup of coffee was waiting at her seat when she returned, and she picked up the menu once more, intending on perusing what looked like a pretty standard diner offering. Except a small blurb at the top caught her attention.

Welcome to the Brick House Cafe, the second oldest building in beautiful, historic Haven Ridge, Colorado.

Haven Ridge, huh? So that's where she was, even if the name seemed to stretch credulity a bit. She kept reading.

Haven Ridge was first founded by Elizabeth Strong in 1880 after her husband died from pneumonia over the long, cold previous winter. The daughter of Massachusetts shipping magnate Ellis Strong, Elizabeth sold the family cattle ranch to her brother-in-law and moved her three children to town to establish the Strong Supply Depot as a stage stop and resupply station for wagons traveling back and forth between the Monarch Mine. It soon became a general store for the large number of farmers and cattle ranchers in the area. The original timber-framed building burned down in 1886 and was replaced by two brick ones—one of which became a restaurant and a boarding house, and then, sixty years later, the Brick House Cafe.

Mallory's mind spun, charmed by the tale and the picture her imagination formed. What a fascinating story, particularly the fact it had been founded by a woman. Why hadn't her research on the area turned up information on Haven Ridge, when it had this kind of history?

"Are you ready to order?"

Mallory jerked her head up at the deep male voice, having momentarily forgotten where she was and why she was here. She flipped over the menu, frantically scanning the entrees, until she finally looked up into the man's dark eyes. "Make a suggestion?"

He lowered his pad. "You feel like breakfast or dinner?"

"You serve breakfast at six o'clock?"

"We serve everything all day. Our most popular breakfast dish is the Liège waffle. It's a true Belgian style with pearl sugar in it—if you've never had it, I highly recommend it." Somehow, he managed to deliver the line with all the enthusiasm of a dentist recommending a root canal. Her worry over her looks was quickly fading into general irritation.

But she still smiled up at him. "Sold. And with a side of eggs, poached medium?"

He scribbled something on his pad and gave a terse nod. "Coming right up."

Mallory stared at him as he swiveled away and disappeared into the kitchen, her brow furrowing slightly. It wasn't as if she expected men to fall all over her, but she might as well have been a bearded trucker in lumberjack flannel for all the interest he had shown in her. It was yet another blow to her ego she really didn't need. The fact that John had dumped her for a woman who was twenty pounds lighter, two cup sizes bigger, and, disappointingly, *not* the bimbo that her proportions would suggest had really done a number on Mallory's self-esteem.

Then again, she had a feeling Amy could have walked in here in a string bikini and this guy would merely have pointed at the sign that said *No shirt, no shoes, no service.* As long as she kept believing that, she could continue fooling herself into thinking she was on this road trip as a way to kick-start her writing career and not because she was fleeing her life in Boise. She could have gone back to Seattle, finished her master's degree, and gone on to the Ph.D. that she needed. She could have moved back to Portland where she was born and raised and where many of her friends had stayed. But that had all felt like defeat, like admitting that the world and her failed relationship had beaten her.

Her eyes traveled back to the blurb on the menu, her mind turning over the story that lay behind those brief words, about a woman who, rather than giving up and moving back east where life was easier, had chosen to stay on the gold rush frontier, make a life and livelihood out of this little isolated spot at the base of the Sangre de Cristo mountain range. Elizabeth Strong couldn't have felt any less defeated than Mallory did, and she'd had three children to consider. Maybe this had been the best way she could think of to provide for them.

Both her personal and intellectual curiosity piqued, Mallory caught the man on his next pass behind the counter. "Excuse me . . . "

He paused, unsmiling, lifting an eyebrow. "Yes?"

"Do you know anything about this? The town history? Elizabeth Strong?"

"Not much more than is written on the menu."

She frowned. "That's too bad. It's an interesting story. Is there anyone else who might know?"

For the first time, he looked at her with more than

passing interest, but she had a feeling that it had nothing to do with personal attraction; rather, he was trying to decide whether or not to waste his time on her. Finally, he said, "My grandmother would know. She's the unofficial town historian."

"No kidding! I came to the right place then."

His brows furrowed slightly and she hastened to explain.

"I'm a writer." Well, it was kind of true. At least for now she was. "I was up here to do a story on Salida, but my GPS malfunctioned and brought me here."

His left eyebrow joined the right one this time. "Salida is another twenty miles down the highway."

Oh. So she was nowhere close. Why in the world had the map made her turn around then?

"Right. Well, let's face it, everyone knows about Salida, but I've never heard of Haven Ridge."

"There's a reason for that. What you see is what's left. The town's been slowly dwindling for as long as I've been alive. The fact that the Brick House Cafe still exists is more a testament to cheap rent and loyalty from the old-timers who still live here."

It was more information than she would have expected from him, though it was no less than she'd guessed herself from her initial drive into town. The thought made her sad. "You grew up here then?"

He gave a nod, then hesitated before he held out his hand. "Thomas Rivas."

"Mallory Adams." She grasped his hand, and his warm fingers closed around hers, sending a pleasant tingle straight up her arm. She caught her breath at the unexpected sensation, saw a flicker of something beneath his stony expression before he pulled his hand away. "I'd love to ask your grandmother a few questions about the town. Is she here?"

"Not at the moment."

"Oh. Then, I don't suppose you could draw me a map of how to get to Salida since my GPS seems determined to take me anywhere but there?"

The expression shifted even more toward wariness, but he nodded anyway. "Coming right up. As is your food."

"Thanks," she said with a smile, watching him walk back toward the kitchen. A few more minutes and she would be on her way, which was exactly what she wanted.

Except that was a lie. She hadn't known what she really wanted in so long, she probably wouldn't recognize it if it were dropped in her lap. All she knew was all the things she couldn't have. And apparently, this town's intriguing story was one of them.

CHAPTER TWO

THOMAS SWIVELED AWAY from the woman at the counter, pushing down the unsettled feeling that had moved in the minute she walked through the door and only intensified the longer she stayed. Granny Pearl would say it was the Strong intuition, which he had inherited from her side of the family, though he would say it was simply because, at thirty-five years old, he could no longer snack on leftover pizza at eleven o'clock at night. And neither of them would be entirely truthful, nor would either of them admit it.

If he were being completely honest, he would admit that seeing Mallory Adams stroll through the door of his restaurant was like being struck by lightning. Every hair stood on end, every nerve ending snapped to attention. And it wasn't just because she was gorgeous, even with makeup smudged beneath her green eyes and her espresso-dark hair slipping out of a messy bun. It was something else entirely. A feeling of . . . inevitability. Of fate, even, if he actually believed in fate. He'd only felt that one other time with one other woman, and he'd married her six months later.

And then it had taken three years for his heart to callous over so that every day didn't feel like a waking nightmare. No matter what his grandmother said about fate, or the Strong intuition, or how he was too young to close off his heart completely, he was never going to go through that again. So Mallory Adams could eat her waffle and take her lightning-strike presence and walk out that door, never to be seen again.

From the kitchen, Arnold called out her order and slid the plates onto the pass-through behind the counter. Thomas whisked them off the pass and carried them over, setting them down carefully in front of her. The Liège waffle was his idea—he'd fallen in love with them when he'd spent his sabbatical in Bruges—and when he'd taken over the Brick House Cafe, he'd put them on the menu. Whereas you could purchase them already garnished in open stands on the street in Belgium, here he served them with three tiny cups of toppings, DIY style: strawberries and whipped cream, Nutella and sliced bananas, and the obligatory American maple syrup. He carefully kept his eyes on the plates, but he still caught her delighted intake of breath when she saw the dish.

"Enjoy," he mumbled and turned away as quickly as possible.

Except as he moved through the restaurant space, checking on the few other occupied tables, wiping down vacant ones, he was acutely aware of the presence of the woman at the counter. He felt her curious gaze on him as he worked, and he took much more time than the tables actually required so he didn't have to talk to her again. The only thing that could be worse than this skin-prickling awareness would be if—

Almost as if he'd summoned her with the thought, he caught sight of a familiar white head bobbing along the sidewalk to the doors. Granny Pearl.

Thomas closed his eyes briefly, steeling himself for what he knew was coming, then swiftly crossed the restaurant floor to meet her at the door. "Granny," he said. "What brings you here?"

She narrowed her sharp eyes at him, not fooled for a minute. "What's going on, Thomas? You look flustered."

Thomas went for diversion. "What happened to your hair?"

Currently, her short silver hair was streaked with pink, though it only barely distracted from her outfit: skinny jeans, a lavender Oxford sporting white cats playing with yarn, and a pair of gray-and-cream Air Jordans she'd bought from a high school kid in town who fancied himself a sneaker mogul. She looked less like a *Pearl* than anyone he'd ever met in his life. No one who didn't know her would ever have guessed she was turning eighty-five this year.

Granny Pearl patted her hair. "Do you like it? Monique talked me into it. I think it's sassy."

"You've got quite enough sass for the entire town," Thomas said, but he softened when she pursed her lips in displeasure. "Of course I like it. It's very you."

"Oh, you." She grabbed his face with both hands and planted a kiss right on his cheek. "Now where's this stranger everyone's talking about?"

Thomas stared in amazement. Mallory had been here less than half an hour, and already word had somehow traveled from the cafe, down the deserted street, and to the gift shop Pearl owned one block over. Even by Haven Ridge standards, that was a record. "She's sitting at the counter. And she was asking about the town."

Pearl's eyes lit up. "Oh, she's pretty."

"Granny," he said warningly.

"I'll be good," she promised, but there was a dangerous

light in her eyes when she sidled over to the counter and climbed onto the seat beside Mallory.

"Hi," she said brightly. "I'm Pearl. I understand you were asking about our town?"

Thomas shook his head, but he couldn't help his smile. She was the reason he'd come back here in the first place. Even though the restaurant technically belonged to Pearl, his grandfather was the one who had run it; after his passing several years ago, she had been disinclined to continue. She already had her shop, and she'd always declared herself not suited for the restaurant business with its long hours and small margins. If it had been anyone else, he wouldn't have believed it when she said she'd only kept it open while she waited for him to come to his senses and take up the family business. But Pearl always seemed to know— call it her great-grandmother Elizabeth's legacy or just the fact that she knew her family better than they knew themselves—and he'd no sooner driven back into town than she met him with the proposal to take over the Brick House Cafe.

Too bad her presentiment didn't extend to how long it would take me to turn a profit, he thought wryly. He was a college professor, not a restaurateur. If he didn't have free rent living in one of the furnished apartments upstairs, he would have given up on it already ... or maybe never taken it on in the first place. Haven Ridge was a small town, getting smaller all the time, and one that barely generated enough business to keep the doors open.

"Oh, I could tell you things about Haven Ridge," Granny Pearl was saying gaily, and Thomas could see that Mallory was delighted by the old woman's enthusiasm. From what he could hear, she was telling Granny about the article she'd been hired to write about Salida, and Granny was doing her best to convince her that she should write the article on Haven Ridge instead.

Good luck with that, he thought wryly. Salida was a hot spot for outdoor sports enthusiasts, especially during the summer, but everyone just cruised right by Haven Ridge. And why shouldn't they? It might have the architecture and the history, but there was precious little to do here in town. Even he had been surprised by how quickly it had dwindled after he'd left home. In seventeen years, it had gone from a thriving, if dinky, village to one step short of a ghost town.

And as much as he wanted to believe that Mallory and her magic pen would be able to bring some interest back to his beloved hometown, he knew that this stopover would just become a footnote, at best a charming anecdote about her trip, and she would be gone just as quickly as she'd come.

CHAPTER THREE

THE OLD LADY WAS A TRIP.

Mallory listened in rapt attention as "Granny Pearl," as she seemed to be known, told her about growing up in Haven Ridge in the 1940s. Had it not been for the extensive web of lines over her face and neck, Mallory never would have believed that the woman was in her 80s, and not just because of the pink streaks through her silver hair.

"But that's not even the most interesting part," Pearl told Mallory. "The most interesting part is how the town even came to be."

Mallory tried to tamp down her excitement, but she was sure it shone through on her face. "Elizabeth Strong."

Pearl nodded sagely. "Yes. You see, my great-grandparents didn't even plan to come this far south in the first place. They actually first settled in Park County, just a couple of hours up the highway."

"Wait ... Elizabeth Strong was your great-grandmother?"

"Yes, of course." Pearl blinked at her as if it was

something Mallory should have already guessed. "Anyway, my great-grandfather Marshall was absolutely certain that they were supposed to settle in Park County because that's where a number of other would-be cattle ranchers were putting down stakes. But Elizabeth was something of a ... well, I suppose we could call her a mystic."

Mallory cocked her head while her fingers itched for a pen to jot down notes. Fortunately, she'd turned on the voice recorder app on her phone so she didn't miss a word. "A mystic?"

Pearl nodded sagely. "She had visions. From God."

"Visions from God?" Mallory was beginning to sound like an echo.

"Oh, I know it sounds absurd now. And it must have sounded absurd back then. Fortunately, Marshall was used to his wife's eccentricities, and they had made him quite a bit of money so far as a gold miner, even when it went against common wisdom. So when she said that they were supposed to go farther down and settle in the Arkansas River Valley, he listened. He and his brother settled large adjacent plots of land just southwest of here and established their cattle ranches."

"And then what happened?" Mallory rested her chin on her hands, the rest of her food forgotten while she listened to the story.

"They were quite successful for a number of years. They lived peacefully with the remaining Ute who had not been resettled to the Western Slope, and it seemed that Elizabeth's visions had been proved out. And then there was a stretch of bad weather that took down fences and sent Marshall out into the pastures for a long period of time. He caught a chill that turned into pneumonia and died early in the winter of 1879."

"But she stayed?"

"That wasn't the plan at first. She had three children, one of whom was my grandfather, all under the age of eight years old. She was going to go back to Boston and live with her parents. But they hadn't approved of the marriage in the first place, and when she wrote to them about her plans, they wrote back and said they didn't have a daughter."

Mallory's hand flew to her mouth to cover her gasp. "How horrible!"

"It was. By that time, she had few options. She knew she couldn't run the cattle ranch by herself, so she sold it to her brother-in-law, Finley. He offered to let her come stay with his family, but evidently, she never got along with Finley's wife. She considered moving to Salida, which by then was established, but like many other boomtowns in Colorado, it was 'a den of vice and iniquity.'"

Mallory could clearly hear the quotation marks in Pearl's tone. She smiled. It probably wasn't that far from the truth. Weren't most of these mining and wagon trail towns simply stops for brothels and saloons, with "respectable" people far on the fringes?

"So what happened then?" she prompted.

"She was desperate for a solution. And according to Elizabeth, she heard a voice say, 'Stay and make a haven for all who need it.'" Granny Pearl's eyes sparkled, her voice taking on a conspiratorial tone. "Well, of course everyone thought she was insane. From what I understand, Finley wanted her to be institutionalized, but he realized that if she was judged incompetent, she might not have been allowed to sell the ranch to him. So his greed saved her. She took her children, packed them up in their wagon, and drove along the wagon trail until she found a likely spot. Then she pitched a tent and got to work."

"That's amazing." Mallory's imagination sparked with the story. What would it have been like to be Elizabeth Strong, defying convention with almost no idea of how she was going to make things work out? "How did she build her depot?"

"That's the most incredible part of the story. Elizabeth stepped out of the wagon, looked to the sky, and said, 'I'm here. This was your idea, so I guess you'd better get to work.' And the next day a miner comes through with two mules and a wagon, looking for employment. He'd been panning farther up on the Arkansas, which was now played out, and like so many of those miners who spent their little bit of gold dust on alcohol and prostitutes, he was now flat broke. So she said, 'If you come and work for me, I'll see you fed and clothed. But none of those vile spirits, and if you even think of fornicating with loose women, I'll drive you out of here with a bullwhip myself.'" Pearl sat back and smiled fondly. "Elizabeth was fearsome with that bullwhip, I'll tell you. She could take the wick off a candle at ten feet."

This story was already beginning to take the form of a tall tale, but Pearl told it with such perfect certainty, it was hard to believe it could have happened in any other way. "And the two of them built the depot?"

"Not just them. Over the next couple of months, more and more people trickled in. And not only men to build the depot, but women and children too, some of them in the same situation as Elizabeth herself. One of them had been a schoolteacher back east, so she set up a school for the children in their one big tent, while Elizabeth oversaw the building. It became a haven for down-on-their-luck settlers who needed a second chance. And within two years, it was a thriving town."

The story was simply enchanting. Real or not, it was

one of those foundational stories that gave life to history, context for the place the town had become. She would love nothing more than to sit here and hear more stories about Elizabeth Strong and Haven Ridge, but it was already getting late, and if Salida was indeed another twenty miles, she needed to be on her way.

Mallory turned off her recorder and placed her hand over Pearl's wrinkled one on the counter. "Thank you so much for sharing. That's one of the best stories I've heard in a long time. I'll see if I can work it into my article. Could I email you if I have more questions?"

Pearl looked at her closely, as if she was trying to determine something, though Mallory had absolutely no idea what. Then she leaned back, dug into her pocket, and pulled out a slightly crumpled business card with the embossed lettering *Haven Ridge Gifts*. It had a phone number and an email address, but no website. "Of course, dear," she said. "Call or email me any time."

Mallory reached for her handbag and slid off the stool. "Thank you again, Miss Pearl."

"Think nothing of it. And please, call me Granny Pearl. Everyone else does."

"Okay then, Granny Pearl. I will."

Thomas appeared at Mallory's elbow and placed a folded sheet of paper on the counter beside her—the map she'd asked for, neatly sketched in pen and labeled in block letters. "I can check you out at the counter if you're ready."

"Oh." She picked up the map and studied it for a moment before shoving it into her purse. "Sure, thanks." She followed him over to the register and handed over her credit card.

"I think you probably made her entire week," Thomas said with a fond smile at his grandmother, who had meandered over to chat with one of the older couples in the booths. "She loves nothing more than talking about her great-grandmother and Haven Ridge."

"It's a fascinating story," Mallory said. "It certainly suits the town name. Even if I don't use it, I think I'd like to write a story on the founding histories of towns in this part of the state. They're always so colorful and entertaining."

Thomas just looked at her with that same assessing stare as his grandmother.

"What?"

He shook his head. "Nothing." He ripped off the receipt from the printer and handed it over to her to sign. She added a sizable tip and signed her name with a flourish. "Safe travels. I hope you're not too late to Salida."

"It was worth the detour," she said, holding his eyes for a moment. He looked away first.

A sign, every much as the one that Elizabeth had gotten from God. She threw him a wry smile, hiked her bag over her shoulder, and headed out to her car. The two couples who had noted her arrival didn't pay any attention to her departure, but to her surprise, the teenage girl was watching her through the window. Impulsively, she raised her hand in a wave and got a surprised smile and wave in return.

Maybe the town wasn't completely dead. After all, the existence of schools—and the lone teenager in the diner—suggested a life beyond the sleepy, mostly shuttered main street.

Mallory settled herself into her SUV with a groan, her back and legs protesting about assuming the position again, and turned the key in the ignition.

Nothing happened.

She tried again. Dead. Not a protest from the starter suggesting a low battery. Not a click from the dashboard that could mean an electrical problem. Just ... nothing. If the key hadn't fit so easily into the ignition, she would think that somehow she had used the wrong one.

"What in the world?" she said out loud. She pulled the hood release and climbed out, circling around front to peer into the engine compartment. The one advantage to having been raised by a mechanic—at least until the age of fourteen—was that she actually had an idea what she was looking at. She started with the most obvious possibility—the battery—checking to make sure that the cables were firmly screwed down to the terminals and had not somehow jolted loose. But both were firmly attached, not even a wiggle to suggest that it was a battery connection issue ... though that certainly didn't rule out the unlikely catastrophic failure of the battery itself. That left the alternator, which could have been going bad for a while and she'd been sucking the battery dry while she was driving, or the starter itself, which was not at all a quick fix.

She looked up and down the street, as if that would make an auto shop miraculously materialize.

"Problems?"

A now-familiar voice made her turn. Thomas stood just outside the door, a bar cloth in hand, still wearing his apron.

"Yeah. Car won't start. I suspect my battery is dead, but I don't know *why* my battery is dead. It's only a year old."

"Want a jump start? My SUV is around back."

"What I'd really love is an auto shop that could test everything. I don't want to get stuck somewhere."

"We have a shop," he said, and her hopes rose, just before they crashed down again. "Opens at nine tomorrow."

The cafe bell tinkled and Granny Pearl came out, smiling broadly. "Car problems?"

"Yes," Mallory said slowly. "It won't start. I probably have a bad battery."

"Or it's just Haven Ridge," Pearl said cheerfully.

Thomas turned to his grandmother. "Granny, stop. You're going to freak her out."

"I'm just saying, it's all a little coincidental. And I believe in coincidences just as much as I believe in Santa Claus."

Mallory chose to ignore that, turning to Thomas instead. "What are my other options here?"

"Well, you can have the car towed to Salida. You were going to be there anyway, and since the town is walkable, you can get your work done while they fix it. But it's going to be expensive."

Mallory thought of the state of her checking account and immediately discounted the tow. She'd dropped her auto club membership to save money, but now she realized that it probably hadn't been the best call right before driving through three states.

"Next option?"

"You can stay here overnight and have it looked at tomorrow morning."

"Like I said, what Haven Ridge wants, Haven Ridge gets," Pearl murmured.

Standing on that sidewalk, in front of a car that was having mysterious mechanical problems and tempted by the legend of a town that by all rights she shouldn't even be in, Mallory got a strange sense of unreality. She wasn't a mystic—not at all—but she did believe that things happened for a reason. And right now, it felt like that reason wanted her here in Haven Ridge.

"Is there a motel around?" she asked hopefully.

"Unfortunately not. The only real hotel was the Monarch, but that's been closed for a couple of years."

Pearl shushed him. "We don't have our guests stay in hotels, Thomas, where are your manners?" She turned to Mallory with a smile. "There's an empty apartment above the cafe you can stay in, if you don't mind a little dust."

Mallory looked at the perfectly normal-looking engine compartment, back at Thomas and Pearl, up to the two rows of gleaming, antique glass windows. And even though she didn't know what it was going to cost her or if she had really gone off her rocker, the first word that came out of her mouth when she opened it was "Okay."

CHAPTER FOUR

IN TRUE GRANNY PEARL FASHION, she dropped a bombshell and then disappeared. Not literally, of course—she said she had left her shop unattended long enough, though they were lucky to get a single visitor in a day, even if she did do a pretty thriving trade in trinkets and antiques on eBay. And Thomas might have believed it if she'd not given him a not-so-subtle wink and then directed him to show Mallory her new digs.

Right now, it was hard to tell which reason was driving his grandmother's enthusiasm more—the fact that Mallory might be persuaded to write an article specifically about Haven Ridge or the fact that she saw a golden opportunity to play matchmaker. Either way, it left him feeling vaguely uncomfortable as he gestured for Mallory to follow him back into the restaurant. "Come with me and I'll show you up."

But Mallory didn't budge, a sudden bloom of pink touching her cheeks. "How much is it? I mean, I already paid for my room in Salida ... "

Thomas stopped, heat rising inexplicably in his own face. "Oh. There's no charge. It's not really ... well, you'll see." He cleared his throat, unsure why he suddenly felt so tongue-tied. "Do you want to grab your bags?"

Mallory looked at him for a long moment, then circled around to the back of her SUV.

He followed her and retrieved a single roller case from the trunk while she pulled out what looked like a laptop backpack, shoved behind stack after stack of plastic tubs and cardboard boxes. Was Mallory homeless?

"Thanks," she said, taking the suitcase from him. "I've got it from here."

He gave a brief nod and led her through the restaurant to a back hallway, where narrow wooden stairs led upward. He passed the first landing with its closed door and the number *1* and continued up another twisting flight.

"I'm sorry in advance," he said.

"About what?" Mallory's breath came out in puffs, but when he reached for the bag, she shook her head again.

"It's been closed up for a while, so it's not exactly . . . rental worthy."

"It's fine," she said. "As long as there's a bed and a bathroom, I'm okay."

Thomas grimaced. Might as well let her see it. She might change her mind about that tow to Salida.

He was pulling his keys from his belt when they reached the top landing, and he bypassed the antique lock that was still on the door in favor of the shiny modern deadbolt that had been installed a few years back. He had to put his shoulder into the door to scrape it free from the frame, and then he stood back to let her enter.

He braced himself for her reaction, but a wide smile spread over her face. "This is charming!"

She turned in a full circle, taking it all in, and he tried to see it as she might. The apartment had all sorts of original detail, from the ornate crown molding to the top-nailed knotty pine floors. He'd always loved the wood-burning fireplace in the corner, with its compliment of Victorian green-glazed tile and iron accents. It was hard to tell the rest, though, because the furniture was covered in sheets. He moved to the nearest piece, a red-upholstered settee, and pulled the covering off.

Mallory dropped her bag and joined him, until the full parlor suite was revealed: two armchairs and an oval central table in addition to the settee. Her smile widened. "How lovely!"

"You might want to reserve judgment until you see the kitchen," he said wryly, leading her through the adjacent door. It was as predictably bad as a 1950s kitchen remodel could be, with flat white cabinets and aluminum-edged Formica countertops. "But I don't expect you'll be doing much cooking, and if you want breakfast or coffee, the cafe is just downstairs."

"It's fine," she said, but he had a feeling that had more to do with beggars not being choosers.

But she seemed legitimately pleased by the bedroom with its carved four-poster bed and matching highboy chest and wardrobe. Someone had recently come up here and changed the sheets, because instead of the dusty brocade bedspread he remembered last, it was covered with a fluffy white hotel-style duvet. He narrowed his eyes. Granny Pearl? But how . . . ?

Best not to ask those questions if you didn't want an answer you might not entirely believe.

"The bathroom is through here." He led her to the door in the corner and watched Mallory's face as she took in the details: pedestal sink, toilet, and a tiny shower cubicle sporting a capped copper pipe where the fixture should have been.

She grimaced. "The shower doesn't work?"

"Afraid not," he said. "But you are welcome to use mine."

She stared at him, and he realized he'd omitted an important detail. "I live in the apartment downstairs. I can leave the door open for you if you like. We close at eight but I've got some work to do in the office, so make yourself at home."

Her dismay vanished, and she favored him with a genuine smile. "Thank you. To you and your grandmother. I appreciate it."

Thomas shifted uncomfortably beneath the warmth of that smile. "You're welcome. I'll let you settle in. If you need anything, you know where to find me."

"Thank you again. Really."

He gave her a quick nod, then turned on his heel and left, closing the door quietly behind him. What was his problem? It wasn't as if he hadn't been around a beautiful woman before, but Mallory's mere presence had him twisted up in knots.

But even as he thought it, he knew the truth. He hadn't even had a woman catch his eye since Estella. Even without Granny Pearl's hopeful look, her certainty that Mallory had come here for a reason that may or may not include him, it felt like a betrayal. And though he knew his wife would never have wanted him to be alone indefinitely, he'd never quite managed to move that conviction from his head to his heart.

So he would help Mallory Adams get her car fixed, maybe nudge her in the right direction to give the town the publicity it so desperately needed, but she was nothing more than a lost traveler who needed their help.

After all, this was Haven Ridge, and they had a legacy to uphold.

* * *

Mallory watched Thomas flee the apartment, downright baffled by his behavior. She'd never met a man who ran so hot and cold in the same minute. She didn't think the attraction between them was one-sided—the look on his face when he'd shaken her hand said that he felt the electrical spark just as surely as she had. But he'd seemed in a hurry to get rid of her, right up until the time that he volunteered to show her the apartment.

Of course, Granny Pearl hadn't given him much choice. The woman was definitely eccentric, but you could tell there was genuine, deep affection between the two of them.

Mallory plopped on the edge of the settee and looked around the room in satisfaction. It might not have been perfect, but it was far and away better than the 70s-vintage motel she'd stayed in last night. She'd worn her leather sandals in the shower, thinking ruined leather was better than whatever fungus she was risking from the shower pan.

Which wasn't going to be a problem here since she didn't even have a shower. And however reluctantly Thomas might offer his own, there was no way she was going to invade his private space unless she absolutely had to.

There was little else to do, so she retrieved her laptop and set it up on the parlor table. She needed to remember to ask if there was Wi-Fi. For the moment, she pulled out her cell phone. Later, she could transcribe her conversation with Granny Pearl so she had a written record of the town's legend. In the meantime, at least she could do a little bit of research on the modern town. Its fascinating history was all well and good, but it didn't help her if the place really was as sleepy and boring as it first appeared from this single street.

Not that Haven Ridge needed to be touristy to be interesting and worthy of its own article. If one opened their eyes, a stunning expanse of culture, a rich tapestry of tradition, was just waiting to be explored. It was, frankly, the curiosity about people and places she carried with her from her history studies that had made her think she could be a travel writer. Every time she read a piece in some travel magazine that told her where to eat and where to shop, she was tempted to roll it up and throw it in the garbage because the writer had missed everything that was actually interesting about travel—the history of places, the traditions of the people, and how it felt to be welcomed into the community, if only for a short time.

Already, she felt like this town might welcome her.

Of course, it was a completely different angle than she had pitched to her editor, though the thing she had come to appreciate about *Altitude* was that they liked to feature hidden gems and out-of-the-way places in their travel section. You didn't get much more out of the way than Haven Ridge.

But it seemed that the internet agreed with her assessment. Other than the town's official page, which looked like it had been created circa 1998, there was precious little available. It was a statutory town in Chaffee County, the seat of which was in Salida—she rolled her eyes at that. It had one elementary school, a middle school, and a surprisingly sizable high school. But other than that, the blurb on the Brick House Cafe menu, and the little bit of history she'd gleaned from Granny Pearl, she wasn't any more enlightened than she'd been when her GPS decided to plop her in the middle of this town. There was a huge gap between the founding of a stage depot, its apparently thriving past if the gorgeous buildings were any indication, and its current sad, failing state.

She leaned back against the settee, nibbling her fingernails while she considered. She still had time to go to Salida. Even if her car wasn't easily fixable, she could always call a cab or a rideshare to take her there. It had to be less costly than a tow to an auto shop twenty miles away. She could write the story that she'd intended, submit it to her editor, move on.

Move on to where? It's not like you actually have a home. A place to live.

She pushed down that little voice in the back of her head, even though it was absolutely true. Digital nomadism had sounded really appealing when it was by choice and not necessity. Just because she could go from place to place writing articles about cities to which she might never return didn't mean she didn't want someplace to come back to.

But she was getting ahead of herself. She still had to make sure that her editor would be okay with her changing her plans, and she wouldn't be able to check in with her until tomorrow. Despite the fact that the local magazine worked with a skeleton staff and an army of freelancers, Bea was one of the few editors-in-chief who truly believed in work/life balance. There was no way she was going to be in the office at eight o'clock on a Friday night. More likely, she'd be out having a drink with her significant other in one of Denver's hip bars.

Definitely not holed up in a borrowed Victorian apartment in a tiny southern Colorado town.

Eight o'clock. Shoot. Her reservation. Mallory reached for her cell phone again, searched for her B&B

confirmation, and dialed what was to have been her accommodations in Salida tonight.

A woman answered the phone after four rings, sounding slightly annoyed at the interruption. Mallory quickly explained her situation.

"I'm sorry," the woman said immediately. "I'm afraid we're completely full tonight."

"No, that's what I'm trying to tell you. I had a reservation. I'm not going to make it, though. My car broke down in Haven Ridge."

"What were you doing in Haven Ridge?"

Mallory shook her head. "Long story. In any case, I need to cancel my room tonight. I'm not sure about the rest of my stay."

"What did you say the name was again?"

"Adams. Mallory Adams."

"I'm sorry, Ms. Adams, we have no record of your reservation."

Mallory was shocked into momentary silence. "That's impossible. I have the confirmation right here."

"Hold on, let me check." Over the line came the clicking of keys. "We have a reservation for Mallory Adams, same date next month. Could you have made a mistake?"

No, I couldn't have made a mistake, Mallory thought, but she didn't say it out loud. If anything, this had just saved her from having to pay for a night's accommodation that she wasn't going to use, a boon to her bank account if ever there was one. "How about tomorrow night? I may be coming into Salida late."

"I'm sorry, Ms. Adams, as I said, we are fully booked. You might check some of the other places outside of town. But it's FIBArk weekend, so you might find that everything else is filled up."

"FIBArk? What's FIBArk?"

"'First in Boating on the Arkansas River.' You know, the whitewater competition? Kayak, raft, paddle-boarding?"

She had no idea what the woman was talking about. How had she missed that one of the biggest events of the summer was going on the weekend she was supposed to be in town writing about the city? It explained why she had been unable to get a reservation in town and had to settle for something on the outskirts. It did *not* explain how she'd gotten bumped to the following month, other than just sheer bad luck.

What Haven Ridge wants, Haven Ridge gets.

As ridiculous as the phrase had sounded, now it took on an eerie kind of sense. After all, she shouldn't be here in the first place. Her usually reliable GPS had somehow malfunctioned so completely that it brought her to the only open business in a nearly defunct town.

She caught the direction of her thoughts and shook her head. What, did she really believe that the town had some sort of sentience? That it had brought her here, canceled her reservation in Salida, and broken her car so she couldn't leave? That sounded like the setup for a bad horror flick, and as sad as this town might be, she knew in her heart that there was nothing malevolent here but the failure of capitalism.

"Ma'am, can I help you with anything else?"

Mallory realized that she was lost in thought while still on her phone call, so she thanked the woman for her time and clicked off, staring for a moment at the phone screen. Ridiculous thoughts or not, her options had just narrowed. If by some miracle her car was fixed tomorrow, she could drive to Salida on Sunday and try to cram a weekend's worth of research into one day.

After all, the festival could be a great feature, even if it did make her pivot away from the "life in a small town" angle she'd pitched.

Or, she could pivot even further and do what it felt like all the events so far were conspiring to make her do. Delve into the past and present of Haven Ridge and hope against hope that her last-minute change didn't get her fired.

CHAPTER FIVE

THE BRICK HOUSE CAFE closed at eight o'clock, but the traffic began to taper off long before then. Most of their business came from the elderly crowd, who tended to eat between four and six, and the high school students didn't want to hang around a stuffy old diner unless there was an event going on at the school ... which, with it being the middle of June, there wasn't. Most likely, they were all hanging out at one of the hot springs, drinking alcohol swiped from their parents' liquor cabinets or bummed off older siblings.

Thomas grinned at the thought as he flipped over the sign and locked the front entrance. He was all too familiar with the things teenagers did in small towns; he might feel old and battered, but his teen years weren't all *that* far off. If he hadn't been trying to convince the prettiest girls in school to go skinny dipping in the springs on a weekend night, he'd been talking his older sister into buying wine coolers, which again were for the pretty girls. Estella, who had grown up in the middle of Chicago, had been horrified by his stories of Haven Ridge weekends. She couldn't conceive of the small-town life, even though it had been relatively innocent by most standards.

This time, the memory of Estella came without the usual pang of loss, bringing only a fond smile. He moved behind the counter to close out the cash drawer for the night, listening to the sound of scrubbing in the back while Arnold shut down the kitchen. He took the meager cash yield back to the safe in his office—even here, most people paid by credit card or on their phones—and sat down in the leather chair behind the ancient oak desk. He was willing to bet that this office hadn't changed since his grandfather took over the restaurant in the 1960s, and despite the slightly yellow-beige paint, Thomas didn't see any reason to change it. The whole place was a time capsule, and there was barely enough money to keep it running, let alone make any improvements.

He'd just tackled the stack of papers in the inbox when the door opened and in stepped Granny Pearl. She'd thrown a leather biker jacket over top of the cat shirt against the evening chill; the oddest thing was not that it looked strange, but that it didn't. She eased herself into the retro—or should he say, legitimately antique?—sling chair in front of the desk and fixed him with a knowing look.

"What?" Thomas asked, putting down his papers.

"Don't use that tone with me, boy. You may be a full-grown man but I can still turn you over my knee if you're going to be disrespectful."

Thomas smiled at the arch tone—mostly put on—and sat back in his own chair. "I'm sorry, Granny. What can I do for you tonight?"

"That's more like it," she sniffed. She narrowed her eyes and studied him. "You know what's going on here, don't you?"

"I'm sorry. I have absolutely no idea what you're talking about." A lie, actually, because he might have the slightest idea what she was talking about.

"The girl! The town brought her here. She's the one."

"The one to do what?"

"The one to save the town! The one to break the curse."

"I'm sorry, did I suddenly step into a Disney movie without my knowledge?"

"You know as well as I do what I mean."

Thomas raised an eyebrow. "I do. Which means that I know as well as you do that there is no curse."

"Hmph. Well, there might as well be. Maybe it's not a curse exactly, but you can't deny that things have been going downhill for years. Ever since that nasty business with the town doctor and how he left his wife and daughter in the lurch. And instead of helping them, what did the town do? It ran them out. That was the beginning of the end, mark my words."

Thomas regarded his grandmother with bemusement, affection swelling in his chest. She really did believe that she had some sort of second sight or intuition or direct line to God as did her great-grandmother before her. And even if he didn't know to what to attribute her uncanny wealth of knowledge, he couldn't deny how often she was right. In this case, though, while he was only vaguely familiar with the scandal she was talking about—since it had happened a couple of years after he'd gone away to college—he was more inclined to believe that it was a reflection on the hard times that had come to the town and not the reason for it.

"Even if it was, what do you think Mallory is going to do about it? She's a writer, yes, but a single article isn't going to turn everything around."

"Don't be so sure. If a single action can bring about a disaster, a single action can bring about a restoration. I know that losing Estella shook your faith, child—"

"We are not talking about Estella," he said, his voice coming out even more clipped than he'd intended. "My wife has nothing to do with this."

Pearl softened and reached across the desk to place her hand over his. "It has everything to do with Estella, child. You lost yourself when you lost her. You lost your faith and your hope and the belief that good things can come out of bad ones. But I see you. I see you coming back to yourself." Her expression turned sly. "I saw the way you looked at Mallory Adams when she wasn't looking."

He felt that flush start on his chest and creep up his neck before he could put a halt to it. That was something that was far beyond his conscious control, the instant feeling of *knowing* when he'd seen her. And if Pearl noticed it, what was to say that Mallory hadn't too?

But Pearl was on a roll. She squeezed his hand hard and looked him directly in the eye. "Why did you even take over this restaurant if you didn't have some hope for the town? If you were just in it for the money, you would have quit as soon as you started."

He didn't have an answer for that. It had been something to do when he moved back, some justification for the fact that he'd left his life behind, quit everything that meant something to him, and basically came home to escape the world. After a while, even in the throes of grief, people expected him to move on. But how could he move on when every part of his life was just a reminder of what he'd lost? He and Estella had worked in the same university; there was not a single corner of the campus that didn't hold her memory. It was impossible to heal when the actions of daily life opened the same wound, over and over again.

As it turned out, Pearl didn't need an answer. "You did it because you knew this cafe was once the heartbeat of the town. It was the first building before there even was a Haven Ridge. And it's been the only continuously running business here for the last hundred years. You brought the town back from the brink of death by saving the Brick House Cafe. And Mallory will be the one to get it on its feet again. You two *together* will be the ones to resuscitate Haven Ridge."

He'd give his grandmother credit for one thing: she did have a flair for the dramatic. Even if he didn't believe for a second that there was any magic underlying the town's foundations, she knew how to appeal to his sense of romanticism, however long buried it might be. He could protest, he could argue, but he knew he'd just end up doing exactly what she asked him to do. So why waste the time?

"What do you want me to do?"

"Nothing taxing," Pearl said airily. "All you have to do is show her around. Show her the things that make Haven Ridge worth saving."

"And what are those exactly?"

She pinned him with a look. "If you need to ask that, then you are not the person for this job. And I'll have to find someone else to show the beautiful, apparently intelligent, undoubtedly interesting Mallory Adams around Haven Ridge."

And darn her if those words didn't spark the tiniest bit of jealousy, just as she'd known they would. This would be a lot easier if she didn't know him so well.

"Fine. I'll do my best. But if this doesn't work, I'm not taking responsibility."

"It'll work." Pearl's tone held the full confidence of a woman with, if not the wisdom of the ages, eighty-four years' worth of observation of human nature. "Just trust me."

CHAPTER SIX

MALLORY HAD BEEN SURE that given the situation—
unfamiliar surroundings, the complete one-eighty on
her subject matter for an article due in just over three
days, the fact that she hadn't been able to fall asleep
without a TV in the background since she was
fourteen—she would be lying in bed all night, staring
at the strange shadows that the light from the street
lamps below cast on her ceiling. Except the minute
that she crawled between the fluffy layers of linens
and sank into the cloud-like mattress, her eyes drifted
shut and didn't open again until she heard the first
strains of birdcall outside in the dim light of
morning.

Mallory rolled over, careful not to dislodge the oh-
so-comfy coverings as she reached for her phone,
which was charging from the single outlet in the room,
only somewhat conveniently located behind the
headboard of the four-poster. A few minutes past six
a.m. It would still be another two hours before she felt
comfortable messaging Bea. Another two hours before
she'd have a firm direction for her weekend.

No doubt Thomas was already hard at work in the diner below, probably catering to the elderly early risers who seemed to be the cafe's main patrons. If she were feeling motivated, she could go down and get her breakfast on. She considered it for a moment, venturing one arm outside the covers before stealing it back in. It might be June, but the mornings were still cold, and that cold seemed to have crept in through the old drafty windows. She remembered seeing radiators the day before, but she suspected that no one had turned them on.

She pulled the covers up to her chin, thinking about how she wanted to order her day, and before she knew it, her eyes had drifted closed. When she opened them next, the light through the windows was no longer the sleepy blue of early morning, but the bright yellow of pure day.

Mallory jerked upright and scrambled for her phone, which had gotten buried in the layers of blankets. 9:08. She'd already lost a chunk of her morning to this blasted cloud of a bed. She threw back the covers and rushed into the bathroom, where she did her best to wash up in the old-fashioned sink with separate hot and cold faucets. There was no way she was going to take Thomas up on his invitation and invade his space, especially when he seemed so reluctant to even speak to her.

She scrubbed her face with a clean washcloth, fashioned her hair into a neater version of the messy bun she'd worn yesterday, and put on a few quick sweeps of makeup—not enough to look like she was trying but enough to hide the fact she'd been in her car for the past two days.

When she was sure she looked at least passably presentable, she shoved her notebook into her handbag, locked the apartment door behind her, and climbed down the stairs to the back corridor of the restaurant. Once more, the restaurant wasn't full, but there were a few more tables occupied than the last time she'd been here, and this time some of them were even under the age of sixty.

She made her way slowly back toward the counter, her spirits lifting the minute she saw Thomas's familiar dark head bowed over the register as he closed out some patron's ticket. As if he sensed her standing there, he lifted his head and greeted her with a cautious smile.

"Good morning. Sleep well?"

"Actually, I did."

"You seem surprised."

"Lifelong insomnia," Mallory said, surprised that she tossed off that little factoid so casually. It was usually something she didn't confess until she knew someone, as if they'd see it as some sort of character flaw.

But he merely nodded. "That sounds unpleasant. You were probably exhausted from all the driving."

"Probably." She slid onto the stool as he came over with a menu. "You didn't steer me wrong with the Liège waffle yesterday, so what do you suggest now?"

"Sweet or savory?"

She thought. "Let's go with savory this time."

He didn't hesitate. "Chorizo breakfast burrito smothered in Colorado green chili."

Just the description made her mouth water. "Done."

Thomas put in the order and came back with a mug and a coffee pot, filling the cup before she could ask. "You look like you could use it," he said, then looked embarrassed. "Sorry, I didn't mean that the way it sounded."

Mallory chuckled ruefully. "I probably could. There's no such thing as too much coffee for me."

"Consider this the first round then," he said, and this time there was a sparkle in his eye. Was buttoned-up, gruff Thomas Rivas actually flirting with her? He inclined his head toward the door. "And if lattes are more your thing, the Koffee Kabin is at the end of the street. They only open eight to five during the summer when school is out. Most of the rest of the town are coffee purists."

"Fair enough." She took a sip of the coffee, which was quite good, and sighed with happiness as its warmth spread through her. "I guess the first order of business is seeing to my car."

"I called the shop first thing this morning," Thomas said. "They're sending over a truck to tow it. So in the meantime, maybe clean out whatever you think you'll need in the next few days."

Mallory grimaced at the words *few days* but she didn't argue. After all, even if they figured out what was wrong, they'd probably have to order parts in—she doubted this tiny one-auto-shop town had parts on hand for a 1997 CR-V. She was going to need to get her editor's buy-in immediately and hope to heaven that she agreed this was a story worth chasing.

"And then after breakfast," Thomas continued, "I thought I could show you the town. Only if you want."

Was it possible that Thomas wasn't actually gruff, but instead shy? The idea suddenly endeared him to her. How could a guy who was that good-looking get tongue-tied talking to someone like her?

She caught his eye with a slight smile. "Yeah, I'd like that. Thank you." She looked around, suddenly realizing something. "But wait, don't you have to—"

"Oh, don't worry. My Saturday hostess is coming in at ten. I just like to handle the breakfast rush myself."

Thomas veered off to seat a group of teenage boys who had just come through the door in a cloud of boisterous laughter and enthusiasm. Mallory pulled out her phone and opened the productivity app that *Altitude* used to communicate with its writing staff. She found the conversation marked *Beatrice Donlin* and typed out a quick message.

My car broke down in Haven Ridge, about 35 miles from Salida, and it doesn't look like I'm going to be able to get over there until tonight at the earliest. What do you think about a piece on a quiet town with an interesting history?

Mallory snapped a photo of the blurb on the menu and attached it to the chat, then set down her phone while she sipped her coffee. But she didn't have long to wait before Bea's message chimed through.

Are you sure there's enough material for a full article? I've got you down for 1500 words. I can't even find Haven Ridge on a map.

Mallory's fingers flew over her virtual keyboard. **I'll know for sure by the end of the day. If I have to, I'll get a rideshare to Salida and cover the whitewater festival this weekend. But I feel like there's something interesting here. I've got the founder's 84yo great-granddaughter on board, and I have a feeling she has some stories.**

This time it took longer for Bea to reply. **Just don't forget that this is a travel article and not a history paper. You need to show why people should actually come here, not just why it's sad nobody knows about it.**

It was an astute observation, and it illuminated Mallory's primary fear about changing her topic. Then again, everyone already knew about Salida. She was just going to have to try extra hard to pitch the idea of a middle-of-nowhere getaway and spin the fact that there were virtually no services as a plus, not a minus.

She'd done harder things, but not by much.

Thomas had disappeared—not that she was constantly tracking his presence or anything—which meant she had a moment to do more internet research on the town. This time she widened her search for the history of Chaffee County that included the word *Strong* or *Haven Ridge* and got a useful hit on a county history website. She scrolled down the page until she got to the section talking about Haven Ridge.

Even though the town had been formed in 1880 and used as a stage depot starting in 1882, it wasn't incorporated into a town until 1901. At that point, they were just considered unincorporated Chaffee County and had used a Buena Vista address even though they were no nearer there than Salida. The current name of Haven Ridge had apparently been taken from the distinctive rock formation that marked one end of town limits, but it had also once been called Haven Springs after the extensive network of hot springs that ran below the whole area. She assumed that somewhere there might be hot springs pools or fountains as there were elsewhere in this part of Colorado, but the map offered no insights.

Mallory clicked a link on the page, which took her back to the town website, which was just as abysmal as she remembered from last night. In fact, only two things were clear from the single page: someone named Doug Meinke was the mayor and quite proud of it, and they should call the Chaffee County Sheriff for non-emergency issues.

So. That was helpful.

But the original history had given her ideas of things she wanted to see, or at least ask Thomas about. If there were still hot springs accessible to the public, that was something that could land it on a worth-visiting list. But there remained a sad lack of accommodations. Maybe there was camping in the area that would appeal to the outdoorsy types? After all, that was as much the target audience for *Altitude* as the hipsters looking for fashionable yet out-of-the-way destinations.

She pulled out her notepad and began to jot a list of things to discuss with Thomas on their tour, which grew longer with each passing minute. She momentarily forgot about the work, though, when the rumble of a diesel engine made her twist on her stool. A wrecker with its dangling hook had pulled up, emblazoned with a peeling logo: *Haven Ridge Auto Repair and Towing.*

She hopped off her stool and fumbled for her keys in her bag, but Thomas beat her to the door, holding it open for her. When they walked out to the curb, a middle-aged man in dark denim coveralls was already standing in front of her car, looking it over.

"Dean Maciolek," he said loudly over the rumble of his truck's engine. He held out a hand before he realized it was stained with grease and dropped it. "Sorry. What's the problem here?"

"Won't start. Won't do anything, actually." Mallory unlocked the door and handed the key over.

"You mind?"

"Not at all."

He leaned in far enough to turn on the ignition and confirm that indeed, nothing was happening. Then he popped the hood and poked around inside a little, doing all the things that Mallory had already checked the night before.

"Could be the starter. Less likely, the alternator. I need to take it over to the shop so I can test it out."

"How much will that cost? The tow, I mean." Mallory hated that she had to be that person, but every time she pulled out her credit card, she cringed at the thought of having to pay it off at the end of the month. She *had* to get this article done.

Dean looked at her strangely, as if she was playing a joke on him. "It's just two blocks from here."

"I know, but—"

Thomas leaned over and murmured in her ear, "He's not going to charge you anything for the tow. That's not the way we do things around here."

Oh. She felt the heat rise to her cheeks yet again, and she was mostly sure it was embarrassment and not the shiver that ran through her at his warm breath on her neck. In her defense, it wasn't as if she was used to people doing anything for nothing, though she shouldn't be so surprised. After all, Thomas and Pearl had given her a place to stay out of the goodness of their hearts.

But then, she didn't exactly know that, did she? Maybe he wanted her to stay and write the article just as much as she needed to. After all, there couldn't be a lot of consistent repeat business for places like the Brick House Cafe and Haven Ridge Auto Repair. Who knew what a little publicity could do for the town?

"Thank you. Do you need my number?"

"Nah. I'll call Thomas when I know something. Okay?"

Mallory flicked a quick glance at Thomas before she nodded. She didn't even know where the shop was, but what other choice did she have? She was going to have to start trusting people sometime. She'd already trusted that Thomas wasn't an ax murderer who had roped his grandmother into luring women to an empty apartment, so turning over her car to a guy who seemed both legitimate and her only chance to get out of here on her own power wasn't much of a stretch.

Within fifteen minutes, Dean had gotten her car out

of the parking spot and its front wheels onto the fold-out towing rack on the back of the wrecker. He scrawled something on a carbon form and then pulled the middle sheet out to hand to her. "Don't worry," he said. "We'll figure out what's going on and get you back on the road soon."

Her inner worries unraveled a little. She nodded and smiled. "Thanks. I appreciate that."

Dean waved and hopped into the driver's seat, then rumbled away, pulling her poor, battered Honda behind him. Thomas turned to her with a reassuring smile. "I bet your burrito is up."

She'd forgotten about breakfast, and sure enough, it was waiting on the pass-through when she took her seat again. She pushed aside her notebook and cut into the burrito with her fork. She nearly rolled her eyes out of her head in pleasure when she tasted it, while Thomas just smiled at her from behind the counter. "Good?"

She was too busy chewing to answer, but she gave him a thumbs-up. She hadn't been so sure about the green chili, but it was delicious and spicy, halfway between a salsa and a gravy. She would eat practically anything drenched in this stuff.

She was halfway through the burrito, though, before she noticed a lingering sense of unreality coming over her. Or no. *Un*reality wasn't the right word. It wasn't that this place felt strange to her or that she felt uncomfortable or worried or any of the other things that should come along with being stranded in a tiny town with no guarantee she'd be able to fix her car, make her deadline, or do any of the other things she'd been fretting over since leaving Idaho. It was that for the first time in longer than she could remember, she felt . . . okay.

It would be too much to call it peace, she thought. But maybe, just maybe, she could call it hope. Optimism.

And that was perhaps the weirdest thing of all.

Thomas came and went, ferrying plates to tables and empty dishes back, as the enormous burrito slowly disappeared. When she thought she could quite possibly eat no more, he slipped behind the counter and paused in front of her. "I just saw Madeline drive up. Let me wait until she settles in and then I'll show you around town."

"Okay," she said, pulling out her wallet. "Let me just pay and we can get going."

Thomas waved a hand. "Don't worry about it. I'm considering you a guest."

She narrowed her eyes at him. "Why?"

He stopped to think. "I don't know," he said finally. "But I think you're here for a reason."

CHAPTER SEVEN

MADELINE TURNED OUT to be a spunky blonde high school student with an almost-terrifying level of efficiency. After she clocked in and tied on an apron, she waved off Thomas like she was the shop owner and he was the employee. "Go. I've got this. I'll call you if we get swamped." The little smirk on her face said how likely she thought that was to happen.

"I guess that means I'm free," Thomas told Mallory with a smile. "Ready for your tour?"

Mallory hopped off the stool and hiked her handbag over her shoulder. "Of course. Lead on."

Thomas held the door open for her, and they both stepped out onto the sidewalk. The earlier chill had fled, leaving in the air the promise of a warm day. Even at just after ten, the sun already held a sting that warned of sunburn when it was fully up—she perhaps hadn't taken the warning of the high altitude seriously enough, especially in the middle of June. She made a note to pick up some sunblock at a pharmacy—if this place even had a pharmacy.

"All right," Thomas said as they started down the

street in the direction she'd come into town. "This is Dogwood Street, which is pretty much the main drag. And this concludes the tour."

Mallory shot him a look, and he answered it with a wry smile. "A joke. Kind of."

She understood the longer they walked, though she'd already noted how empty this street looked. Many of the buildings had their windows boarded up—to protect against weather, Thomas explained, not crime—and even when there were businesses present, most of them weren't open yet this morning. There was a Chinese restaurant across the street with its shades down and printed menus in the window. A few buildings farther, there was a thrift store with a sad-looking assortment of toys in the window and peeling letters on the sign above the door. On the corner, one of the three-story brick structures had been converted to a professional building, which seemed to house a doctor, a dentist, and an attorney that may or may not have still been practicing.

"What happened here?" she asked. "It looks like it was thriving once."

"It was," Thomas said. "When I left seventeen years ago, every single one of the buildings was filled. We had everything we really needed on a daily basis. But then kids started leaving and not coming back from college. There's only so long a town can survive with people going out and not returning."

"But surely that's not everyone," Mallory said. "There's obviously schools, so some people are having kids and coming back."

"Sure, a few people have. People getting priced out of the housing market in Los Angeles and Denver and Portland and New York. Anyone who can work remotely can afford a nice house here, even if they have to drive a while for anything fancier than a diner. But they're not opening businesses because there's not enough people to support them."

Mallory sighed, thinking over the catch-22 in her head. It was sad, seeing these old historic towns slowly fade as people moved into the cities. It was like an entire way of life was being lost. They might not be so far from civilization, but there was something beautiful and rustic and lonely about this part of Colorado, not quite desert and not quite mountain, that appealed to a certain type of individual. She glanced at Thomas, trying to fit him into the mold that she'd just cast.

"Why did you come back?"

He was quiet for a long moment, and Mallory wondered if she'd said something wrong. Finally, he cleared his throat. "My wife passed away three years ago."

Mallory sucked in her breath and then dissolved into a coughing fit that had Thomas patting her consolingly on her back. When she could speak again, eyes watering and throat raw, she croaked, "I'm so sorry. I didn't mean to be nosy."

"It's okay," he said quietly. "Everyone here knows. I'd almost rather people just talk about it outright than tiptoe around it, but no one knew Estella, so I think to them, it feels like it didn't happen."

Mallory met his eyes, regretting her faux pas. Three years was certainly long enough to grieve but not forget, but his eyes now were clear, his voice steady. "What was she like?"

He smiled, almost as if her question was a relief. "Smart. Beautiful. She and I met through mutual friends in Dallas. We were both college professors at the time, and I think our friends thought it would be amusing to stick us together in the same room and then step back to watch what happened."

Mallory's forehead creased. "Why was that?"

"Because she taught physics and I taught art. They figured we'd get into a left brain/right brain grudge match. But as soon as we started talking, we had a connection. We understood each other. She was raised by first-generation immigrant parents from Mexico, and one side of my family came here from Cuba in the fifties. We both had a great appreciation for the religious traditions of our families as well as open-mindedness from working in academia. To say our friends were disappointed that we left the party together to go have dinner someplace quieter would be an understatement."

Mallory smiled at the obvious affection and nostalgia in Thomas's voice. "That sounds a bit like a fairy tale," she murmured, "or a romance novel."

Thomas chuckled. "That's what everyone else said. We got married six months after we met, and there were the usual whispers that it would never last. Imagine how bad they felt when they learned the reason why it wouldn't last." Even though his voice was light, there was a thread of pain beneath. She sensed that he wanted her to ask.

So she did, though she focused her gaze on the cracked sidewalk beneath their feet and not on his face. "What happened?"

"Cancer. Diagnosed six months into our marriage, stage three. She fought it for a long time, but in the end ... " He cleared his throat once more, which she was learning was a sure sign he was uncomfortable or hiding emotion. "She died nearly three years to the day we met. So I've officially been without her for as long as I knew her, and it feels strange that such a short period of time could have made such an impact."

"When you find your person," she murmured, "time isn't measured in regular terms."

He smiled. "I suppose that's true. Anyway, I'm sorry to dump that on you. We just met and you hardly wanted to hear about my personal tragedies."

"No," she said quietly, stopping so she could look him in the eye. "It's okay. I understand what it's like to be grieving a loss when everyone else has already moved on. My parents died in a car accident when I was fourteen. I went to live with my mom's cousin, and she was nice enough, but I think she thought it was better for me to just forget what happened and get on with life. All I ever wanted was for her to talk about her memories of my parents, but she never would."

Thomas looked at her closely, something in his expression shifting imperceptibly. "I'm sorry. I can imagine how hard that must have been."

"Yeah," she said, holding his gaze. "I'm sure you can."

The moment stretched, and then he broke the gaze and started walking again.

"I'm curious though," Mallory said finally. "I can understand needing to get away from your old life. But you could have gone anywhere. Why here?"

"I don't know. I suppose when I came back for a visit, it felt natural."

"Because you grew up here?"

A wry smile touched his lips briefly before it disappeared. "Because it reflected how I felt. Like everything was falling apart. The future hadn't been what I expected for myself, and it hadn't been what the town had expected either. And I guess ... it felt like it needed me. When my grandfather died and Granny Pearl wanted to shut the cafe down, it was like the original family—even though he wasn't a Strong—was giving up on Haven Ridge. And that felt wrong."

"That's romantic," she said with a smile, darting a glance at him. "Must be exposure to all that art."

He opened his mouth to speak, but before he could, Mallory caught sight of the building in front of which they were passing. The shiny, crystal-clear windows were hung with paper flowers, framing a beautiful vignette of elaborately-frosted cakes on what appeared to be antique milk glass stands. Mallory stopped sharply and looked at the sign hanging above the door: *Sugar Dreams*.

Without consulting him, she reached for the door and stepped into the cool space, fragrant with the aroma of sugar and strawberries and cocoa. A large case displayed cookies, muffins, and cupcakes behind the register, and a hand-lettered chalkboard displayed prices on the back wall.

The tinkle of the bell on the door brought a man from the back, wearing a flour-smudged apron and wiping his hands on a towel. "Oh, hey, Thomas," he said easily. Then his eyes lit on Mallory, taking a second to clock the fact he didn't know her. "Welcome to Sugar Dreams."

"Mallory, this is Jayden. He owns this place. He supplies the diner with coffee cake and pies and such. For now at least."

Mallory looked between Thomas and Jayden. "For now?"

Jayden gave a rueful smile. "I'm in the process of moving back east," he said. "My wife got a job in D.C. and they're not allowing remote work like her old company."

"That's too bad," Mallory said. "What does she do?"

"Software engineer."

She enjoyed the gender-flip for a moment before the rest of it sank in: the idea that this lovely little space, this bit of sugar and light on an otherwise dwindling street, was going to be gone. She looked at Thomas. "What are you going to do for baked goods then?"

"I haven't figured that part out yet." Thomas threw a helpless look at Jayden, who returned a regretful grimace.

Well, she couldn't do anything about that, but she could at least buy something. She stepped up to the case and perused the baked goods. She was going to be here for a couple more days, but she'd definitely need something for the road. She settled on a dozen assorted mini cookies in various flavors, which Jayden packed in a white pastry bag and handed over the counter. After she paid and they said their goodbyes, they slipped back out on the street and she tucked the cookies into her purse.

"That's a shame," she said as they started walking again. "It's one of the few places that seems to be thriving and it's closing?"

"To be fair, anytime you have students, a bakery is going to do well, but yeah. I haven't quite figured out how to replace his pastries. I might have to bring things in from Salida or Buena Vista or even a food service supplier."

Her wrinkled nose conveyed her feelings on the last option.

He laughed. "I do have Granny Pearl's famous pecan pie recipe. It's the only thing we make in the restaurant because she would never give the recipe to someone who wasn't family. Fortunately, she taught me how to make it when I was a kid, so it's the one hands-on thing I actually do there. If it weren't for Arnold, we wouldn't have a restaurant."

They'd reached what seemed to be the end of the commercial part of the street, terminating in a large park on the corner. The tall oaks and pines and spruces brought a green counterpoint to all the reds and browns of the buildings, a lush green lawn stretching out around a sandy play area. A few children were running around under the watchful eye of two women, who were chatting on a park bench.

Mallory smiled. A few minutes ago, she was wondering why on earth Thomas would have left Dallas to come back here, but that was before she saw the small spots of life in the town, like the first spring flowers pushing up through a crust of snow. Everything might have looked dead from the outside, but now she wondered if it was just dormant, waiting for some tender care and spring rains to bring it back to life. She might have accused Thomas of being romantic, but that was a romantic thought if she'd ever heard one.

"What's that?" she asked, pointing to what looked like a stone monument in the middle of the park.

"Oh, that's the spring fountain." He cast a glance at her. "Come on. I'll show you."

They cut a path across the grass to the stone structure, Thomas raising a hand in greeting to the women, but he didn't pause until they were standing before it. Now that they were close, Mallory could see that there was an indentation in the stone column that held a copper sink bowl and a green-tinged spigot directly above it. "Go ahead," he said. "Try it."

Mallory gave him a quick doubtful glance, then twisted the spigot on. Immediately a slow flow of water trickled out, which she caught with her hands.

"It's hot!" she exclaimed in surprise. Not hot enough to burn, but definitely warmer than she'd been imagining, even after having read about the town's original name. She scrubbed her hands briefly beneath the water, then cupped some in her palm and brought it to her mouth. It had a distinctly mineral taste to it, like drinking hot, flat Perrier. She twisted off the faucet and shook her hands dry. "That must feel really nice on a winter's day."

Thomas grinned. "It does. And of course, the fountain never freezes like the others."

That was the perfect segue into the other thing she wanted to ask him. "I was a little unclear on where else you could access the springs. Wasn't there a bathhouse at one time? Is it still open?"

"There was," he said, and the reluctance in his voice warned her about the bad news before it came. "It closed down about ten years ago. The town didn't really have the money to maintain it—the mineral content is really hard on the pipes—and so they capped the source. It's permanently locked up, though we can walk by later if you want to see it."

"But surely there are other places you can access the springs."

A mischievous sparkle appeared in his eye, and even though she didn't know the source of it, it made something inside her flutter in anticipation. "There is. But it's a bit of a drive. I can take you later if you feel like a ride."

"Not now?" she asked, disappointed. An idea was already forming in her mind for the direction of her article, and the springs were a big part of it. She didn't want to waste time on other things if she had something to definitively pitch to Beatrice and get her buy-in before she even started writing.

But that look just intensified. "And let you miss out on the rest of what Haven Ridge has to offer? You're just going to have to be patient."

CHAPTER EIGHT

IF THOMAS SENSED MALLORY'S DOUBT fading when she stepped into Sugar Dreams, he knew the fountain was the turning point. It was almost as if he could tell the moment that she began to see the town through his eyes; not as a tourist who had come to a place and found it to be disappointing, but as someone who might understand why Haven Ridge would be such an appealing place to live.

He knew because he'd gone through the same transformation himself.

Yes, he'd grown up in the town, but what young boy—and later teenager—could appreciate the things that would make his place of birth an appealing home? He'd always seen the whole area as hopelessly rural and boring. They had to drive almost two hours to Cañon City when they wanted a real town, and even farther to Colorado Springs if they needed big city amenities. When he'd gotten a chance to go to school in St. Louis, he'd jumped on it. Maybe Missouri wasn't exciting like California or New York, but it was an honest-to-God city with real restaurants and malls and multiplexes.

When he'd finished his master's degree in Fine Arts and gotten a job teaching in Texas, Dallas was even more of a revelation ... even if Chicago-born Estella had laughed at his provincial naivete, especially considering how eloquent he waxed about old masters hanging in museums he'd never been to.

But when she'd died, he'd realized the things that he'd loved about a big city—the life, the anonymity— only made him feel more alone. He started longing for things like narrow historic streets, the hot springs pools, even the Winter Festival that the high school put on in its parking lot every February. People who had known him his whole life. Not having to explain himself every time he met someone new and they wanted to know why someone of his age wasn't married yet.

And he could almost see that same shift in Mallory the longer they walked together.

But maybe it wasn't just the town. He didn't know why he'd unloaded his whole history with Estella as he had, but he'd seen the empathy in her eyes. Not sympathy—he'd had enough sympathy for the last three years. But deep understanding. And when she'd told him about losing her parents as a teenager, there was still enough pain evident in the telling that he knew that finally, here was someone who understood.

"So what else is there to see?" Mallory asked, as they left the park behind and he turned her down an intersecting street—Florida Avenue—to loop back into town.

"I guess that just depends. Architecture or amenities?"

"Architecture."

For that, they'd go back toward the center of town, where block upon block of historic buildings sat primly upon the Haven Ridge grid layout. He stopped in front of particular buildings of note—glad he still remembered the project he'd done his senior year on the town's important buildings—and gave her what background he remembered. There was the bank, which still functioned as a bank; it was the fourth oldest site in town, but had been rebuilt from its original frame-and-timber structure at the turn of the twentieth century. Unlike the others, this wasn't built into a row but rather took up an entire corner of California Avenue and Columbine Street, its granite facade and Renaissance Revival-style architecture as impressive as the Denver Mint building upon which it had been modeled.

Then there was a boardinghouse—now vacant—that Elizabeth Strong had established specifically for single or widowed women with children, presided over by a landlady with an in-house governess that allowed the women to work when the children weren't in school. The whole time, Mallory scribbled notes in her notebook beneath the building address, noting the number on her camera roll whenever she took a picture. She might have been the most organized journalist he'd ever seen.

When he said as much, she gave a self-conscious laugh. "That's what five years of studying history gets you."

He stared at her. "You're a historian?"

"I was going to *be* a historian."

"So why weren't you?"

"*That* is a story for another day, and maybe another six months of acquaintance," she said lightly, but there was something darker beneath the words. He didn't press. Some things weren't his business, and as she just gently reminded him, he'd known her for less than twenty-four hours.

Except it felt like much longer. Other than with his late wife, he'd never felt so comfortable in a woman's presence so quickly. As she'd probably already guessed, he'd spent most of his life being painfully shy for no good reason. Maybe it was because of his two outgoing sisters who did most of the talking, or maybe it was just because he'd always preferred his art supplies to the presence of other people. But after the initial awkwardness had worn off, he had realized that he and Mallory shared a surprising amount in common. Both of them had had painful loss in their lives; both of them had studied for a career in which they were ultimately not working. And, if he wasn't mistaken, both of them felt that current of attraction underpinning their interactions, which they were valiantly trying to hide by not touching and keeping a safe distance on the sidewalk.

"Where's the original school then?" she asked, and it took him a moment to unwind what they'd been talking about before their conversation—and his internal monologue—had gone off on a tangent.

"Oh, it's just outside of town on the far side of the highway. It was placed there purposely to allow the ranch kids to attend in the morning without having to come all the way into town."

"So how did the town kids get there?"

"Wagon," Thomas said with a smile. "Every morning, one of the mercantile employees—Elizabeth's employees—would load up the kids in the wagon, packed shoulder to shoulder like sardines, I would imagine, and take them to school. And every afternoon, someone would go pick them up and bring them back."

"And Elizabeth did all of this?"

Thomas nodded. "That's the story. Being a widow herself, she understood the need to work while getting her children an education. She herself had been edu- cated by tutors and governesses, so even considering that the schooling of a society lady might have been less comprehensive than that of her brothers, she must have still been a well-educated woman."

"Is there anything documenting this somewhere?"

He thought for a second. "I'm sure there are records at the county historical society."

"Which is where?"

He threw her a wry smile. "Buena Vista. Opposite direction from Salida."

She rolled her eyes. "It figures."

"Most of this I just learned from Granny Pearl. Apparently, Elizabeth loved this town more than nearly anything and she drilled its history into her children and grandchildren—"

"Who continued the tradition."

He gave a nod. "I guess Elizabeth Strong served on the town council until she was in her nineties. She didn't count on anyone not messing anything up without her. Which, if you look at things now, I guess she had a point."

"Sure," Mallory said reasonably, "but sometimes that's just the life cycle of a town, right? It's sad, but people move out and move on, and there's just not enough to sustain the businesses that were there before and it fades away. It's not like anyone 'messed it up' as you said."

Thomas hesitated as Granny Pearl's words came back to him. *You can't deny that things have been going downhill for years. Ever since that nasty business with the town doctor . . . That was the beginning of the end, mark my words.* He truly didn't believe in curses. But he couldn't deny that actions had consequences.

Mallory picked up on his conflict. "What? What is it?"

He started walking again, trying to think of a way to phrase it without her thinking he was completely off his rocker. Or more likely, that Pearl was off her rocker. "So the name, Haven Ridge ... "

Mallory glanced at him, her eyes suddenly bright and interested.

"It's not just a name. You see, the town was founded to be a literal haven. Elizabeth declined to move to one of the gold rush boom towns because it was so dangerous for families. She founded this place as an alternative to Salida, for example. No alcohol, no gambling, no weapons allowed inside town limits." He slid her an amused smile. "She even managed to convince a down-on-his-luck gunfighter to be the town sheriff to enforce the laws. And you can see it in all the provisions the town made: the boardinghouse, the school wagons, the fact that she herself opened a milliner's and dressmaker's shop to employ the women in town that needed jobs—who were of course some of the shop's patrons. It was a closed loop. What was good for the people was good for the businesses was good for the town."

"And over time, it lost sight of that?"

"All places have an ebb and flow, but Granny Pearl is convinced that a particular nasty bit of town shunning right after I left hastened its demise."

Mallory was looking like she was struggling with the idea. "And do you believe that?"

"Do I think there is some sort of karmic debt to be paid?" He glanced at her. "No. I don't. But do I think that shame and guilt can do a number on a community? Do I think that one selfish action can cascade into more selfish actions until everyone is just looking out for themselves? Yeah. I do."

It wasn't until the words left Thomas's mouth that he realized he believed what he was saying. There were still good people here, individually. But maybe what they'd forgotten was how to be a community. How to be proud of what Haven Ridge stood for.

And maybe, just maybe, all they needed was a kick from an outsider.

"I need to think that over," Mallory murmured. "I'm not sure exactly what to do with that."

Thomas nodded, but he sensed he was losing her. So he reached for the one thing that he knew would get her back, reignite the interest in the town.

Because however he had tried to deny his grandmother's premonition about Mallory's importance to Haven Ridge, he was beginning to think that she was right.

CHAPTER NINE

"A PICNIC?" Mallory stared at Thomas, wondering if she'd heard correctly. "We're going on a picnic?"

Thomas stared at her from behind the counter as he packed the sandwiches that Arnold had made them in a bright blue cooler, along with containers of side dishes and several glass bottles of soda. "What? You're acting like you've never gone on a picnic before."

"I haven't," Mallory said before thinking about how it sounded, earning a look of disbelief from her de facto tour guide. "I mean, I've taken sandwiches and things to eat at the park, but not a real ... " She waved her hand and broke off, realizing that it made her sound completely pathetic. *Hi, I'm Mallory, I haven't even done the most rudimentary fun things.*

To be fair, before her parents died, that really hadn't been their thing. They'd go on road trips and eat at greasy spoon diners and truck stops, which in and of themselves were an adventure. They'd go ice skating at the local rink. They'd ride their bikes to the grocery store in the rain, where they got cups of hot cocoa from the deli counter and drank them dripping in the store vestibule while steam rose off their clothing. And after that ... well, Aunt Rita really didn't want to be reminded much that she was now responsible for a teenager, and besides, Portland wasn't exactly a picnic-y sort of place most of the year.

"A picnic," she repeated, giving a nod. "Okay then."

A wide smile broke out over Thomas's face, and she realized that he'd really been concerned about her reaction. He was warming up to her. The way that he'd given a tour of the town, full of enthusiasm and knowledge, like he was trying to impress her, was undeniably endearing. It was like he didn't realize that he didn't have to prove himself; women were no doubt drawn to him just because of what he looked like and who he was. But she'd be willing to bet he'd spent his entire childhood being shy and retiring and his brain hadn't quite caught up to his adult reality yet.

The thought that maybe he'd married Estella because she was the first one to make him feel important made her a little sad. Not that she knew anything about his relationship, and she wasn't going to minimize the impact that one's spouse dying could have on a person, but she wondered how much of his grief was about losing the one person he thought could count on to love him and not about the six months they'd spent before they lived under the shadow of her cancer.

And now she was psychoanalyzing someone that she didn't even know, when she had no qualifications for doing so. Except for the fact that now, seeing him so eager to please, made her think that maybe she was right.

He closed the hamper, murmured something to Madeline behind the counter, and then gestured for Mallory to follow him down the back corridor toward the restroom. Instead of taking the staircase up to their apartments, he instead headed straight for the door marked *Exit* that let them out into an alley parking lot behind the cafe.

"This is me," he said, unlocking a late-model maroon SUV with his key fob. He popped the rear liftgate to load the cooler, and she caught a glimpse of folding chairs in bags, a couple of blankets, and a big battered duffel. When he saw her looking, he explained with a smile, "Emergency supplies." She wasn't entirely sure whether he was serious or not.

He circled to the passenger door first to open the door for her, and she gave him a surprised little smile as she stepped onto the running board and slid into the leather seat. He closed the door behind her, enveloping her in the scent of cinnamon and vanilla. The smile widened when she saw the little wooden artist's palette hanging from the rearview mirror. Gorgeous, gruff, shy Thomas Rivas was an enormous geek.

Thomas climbed into the driver's seat and saw her looking at it. His cheeks colored slightly. "My niece, Allison, gave that to me. She made it in arts and crafts at school. It's supposed to be a Christmas ornament, I think."

"That's sweet. How old is she?"

"Eleven. My oldest sister's daughter. Only child and spoiled like you wouldn't believe. Except not spoiled as in ruined. She's a sweetheart."

The genuine affection with which he talked about his niece brought a smile to Mallory's lips again. "Do they live here?"

He shook his head. "No. Irene and her husband— and Allison, of course—all live in Albuquerque. And my younger sister, Adele, lives in New Jersey and works in Manhattan."

"Wow, so you're it for Haven Ridge?"

He twisted to back out of the parking space and slid the car into drive. "Except for my grandmother on my mom's side."

He'd brought up his mom, so that made the next question fair game. Besides, she'd already told him about hers. "What about your parents?"

"They retired in Spain. Well, not retired exactly. My father's a musician. A flamenco guitarist. So it was kind of an obvious move."

"So you got the artistic temperament from your dad."

"Something like that. And a tolerance for risk and sense of impracticality from my mom." He threw her a wry look as he navigated the SUV through town. "Let's face it, art is not exactly known to be a money-maker."

Mallory grinned. "Yes, because people study history to become millionaires."

"Good point." Thomas laughed. "How did you end up studying history? Was it always an interest for you?"

Mallory settled back against the seat. "I suppose it must have been. I loved books and movies about the Old West and the Oregon Trail, even as a kid. It seemed so ... adventurous. Then, of course, there was the year that I dressed only in prairie skirts and wore my hair in braids and—I'm embarrassed to admit—imagined myself as a long-suffering ranch wife defending her acreage against land-jumpers and neighbors trying to steal her water rights."

Thomas broke into a full-throated laugh, darting a glance at her as he drove. "So it was the stories that did it for you."

"Probably." She smiled, but it quickly faded. "That was the year my parents died. I think I was desperate to escape into anything that wasn't my current reality." She shrugged and made her voice light. "At least it had a career path attached, right?"

Thomas slowed as they approached the intersection with the highway, and when the SUV came to a stop, he placed his hand over hers where it rested between them on the console. "I'm sorry, Mallory."

Her breath caught at the touch of his hand over hers, the warmth of his fingertips, and she jerked her gaze up to meet his. She knew he'd meant it as a comforting gesture, empathy from someone who understood her grief, but now something else sparked in his dark eyes, awareness of the sudden pull of gravity between them. Almost as of one mind, they pulled their hands back into their laps, and Thomas accelerated onto the highway.

"Anyway," Mallory continued, cursing the sudden tremor in her voice, "what started out as an escape turned into inspiration. This whole part of the country was settled by people with few resources other than their own determination and hard work. And so I thought, if they could make lives for themselves with so little, what could I do when I had so much? And what could other people do if they understood the stories of those that came before them?"

"Like Elizabeth Strong."

"Like Elizabeth Strong," she agreed.

Mallory fell quiet, watching the desert-like landscape slide by outside the window as they headed into the hills that bordered the town. After a few moments, Thomas said quietly, "I'm sure your parents would be proud of you now."

The words hit with a pang of regret. "I'm not so sure about that. I've made so many mistakes lately that they're probably looking down on me and shaking their heads."

"No," Thomas said, sliding her a brief look. "They're probably thinking how proud they are that despite everything you've been through, your ambition is to inspire other people to overcome and achieve. That hardship made you strong and not selfish."

She flushed at the words, even while she wondered when she'd become such a blusher. It was a kind assessment, especially from someone she'd just met, and her first impulse was to brush it off. "I don't know about that."

"I do. And someday, when you look back, you'll see how all the things that didn't make sense or seemed like mistakes brought you to where you needed to be."

It was a romantic notion, but maybe she shouldn't be so surprised when it came from someone who had taught art for a living. She would have said as much, but she was suddenly distracted by the scenery outside her window. She'd thought that they were going *up*, but now it seemed like they were going *through*, threading a dirt road through the hills to a little hidden valley. After a few minutes, Thomas pulled the SUV to a stop in a wide circular pull-out beside a crumbling split-rail fence.

"This is it?"

"Don't look so impressed," he said wryly. "Just wait."

They hopped out of the car, and Thomas handed her one of the quilted picnic blankets from the back of the vehicle while he grabbed the cooler. "Hope you don't mind a bit of a hike."

"Not at all," she lied, and he laughed because her thoughts were so evident in her voice.

"Don't worry. It's not very strenuous."

Maybe not for him, but she hadn't planned for a hike when she'd put on her strappy leather sandals that morning. It wasn't even a proper trail, but a steep path worn through a sweep of native grasses, punctuated by evergreens and succulents, so narrow that they had to walk in single file. Every once in a while, the path intersected a boulder or a rockfall, and Thomas would climb up first and then offer his hand to help her up behind him.

Merely a chivalrous gesture, of course, but every time his fingers closed around hers, it felt like grasping a live wire, a little buzz of electricity traveling through her and making her heart beat a little faster.

Don't be stupid, she told herself. *You're just feeling the effects of all the oversharing. It doesn't mean anything.*

Except it seemed like each time they touched, it took a little longer for Thomas to release her hand.

And then the trail ended abruptly, emptying into a flattened-out area scattered with huge boulders and a pond about the size of a small swimming pool. Tufts of wild grasses marked its pebbly margins, the sloping sides shifting the color swiftly from crystal clear to a dark grayish-green. If it weren't already so warm, she imagined there'd be curls of steam rising from the water's surface.

"Here we are," Thomas said, guiding her to a sandy spot that looked like it had been used for picnics since time immemorial, right on the edge of the pool. He took the blanket from her and spread it out. "This is Mason's Spring."

Right. Information for her story. She needed to remember why she was here—and it wasn't to hold hands with a man she'd just met, however objectively gorgeous he might be. She pulled herself back to a more professional mindset. "*Mason* as in a person or *mason* as in a profession?"

"I have no idea, actually. I'm not even sure that's its real name. It doesn't exist on any map."

"So this is your secret personal hot spring?" A note of flirtation had crept into Mallory's voice without her permission. Fail. Again.

"More like an entire town's personal secret hot spring," he said with a grin. "There are other bigger ones up the highway, and they are on a map. But this one ... you have to know how to find it."

"Close enough." She plopped herself on the blanket and crossed her legs. She really wasn't hungry yet after that huge breakfast, even considering all the walking they'd done this morning, but she also wasn't going to turn down what looked like a very nice lunch. Thomas started unpacking all the things he'd brought: some lovely caprese sandwiches on soft Italian bread, pasta salad, an assortment of cut fresh fruit, and flavored sparkling water. She accepted the plate that he handed her—real stoneware from the restaurant—and settled it in her crossed legs with a smile.

"This is fun," she said. "Thanks."

He caught her eye and held it for a long moment, long enough for her to realize she was holding her breath. Waiting ... for something. And then the moment passed, and he was making his own plate with efficient motions. He settled beside her and set his plate in front of him on the blanket.

The food was delicious, just as everything else from the restaurant had been, and they ate in silence for several minutes, listening to the rustle of the wind through the trees, the answering calls of birds above them, the buzz of bumblebees circling the wildflowers that dotted the clearing. The smell of dusty foliage and pine filled her senses, joining the flavors of the food in a not-unpleasant medley.

"I can almost see why people like camping," she admitted. "There's something relaxing about doing ordinary things surrounded by nature." That reminded her of the questions she had yet to ask about the area, but she was reluctant to break the peaceful interlude with business. This outing had stopped feeling like Thomas's attempt to impress her with Haven Ridge's offerings and turned into something more personal.

"I know what you mean," he said thoughtfully. "I think that's why artists have always been so enthusiastic about painting *en plein air*. It's sort of like the boundaries between you and the environment get erased."

There was something about the way he said it, a wistfulness, that made her ask, "You're a painter?"

"*Was* a painter."

The emphatic answer said that avenue of conversation was closed, even if it only piqued her interest. She knew he had taught art at the university level, but she hadn't been sure if that meant fine arts or art history. She hadn't processed that he himself was an artist. But now it all made sense. She didn't have to read between the lines to guess that when Estella had died, he hadn't just lost his wife but his enthusiasm for his art as well. It was hard to keep teaching something you could no longer bring yourself to do.

The realization made her want to reach across the space between them and cover his hand with hers, but she chickened out, even though he'd already done the same thing. He'd think it was only sympathy she was feeling and not connection; he couldn't possibly know that she found these moments of vulnerability appealing. She'd never known what was going on in John's mind or heart; he'd thought that was weakness. That was why she hadn't had any idea that he was no longer happy in their relationship.

Or maybe he had never been happy in their relationship.

"I'm homeless right now," she blurted.

He stared at her, as well he should, given the lack of lead-in.

"My boyfriend and I broke up and he took our apartment. Well, it was always *his* apartment, I realize now, no matter how much he said it was ours. So I took this assignment, packed my things, and drove to Colorado."

Thomas stared at her, and she realized how pathetic it sounded. She had a tiny SUV and he'd seen what was in her trunk. The fact that those were all her possessions in the world had probably finally tipped him off that she was not a real functioning grown-up human being, but still that child who had gotten shunted off to her aunt's house with only the possessions she could fit in a single suitcase.

But there was a sort of appreciative glint in his eye when he said, "You're brave."

She frowned. "What?"

"Well, when I had my crisis, I ran home to my grandmother." He threw her a crooked smile. "You packed up all your stuff and didn't look back. I think that's brave."

"Hardly," she said. "I'm running away."

Thomas shook his head. "Call it a change of direction. Sometimes we glamorize sticking it out when it's not the best thing for us. I don't regret coming back here even though it hasn't been easy. Even though those rather expensive college degrees are going to absolutely no use while I run a family restaurant." He threw her a wry look that said he guessed she shared that feeling.

Mallory looked down at her hands, afraid to see what was in his eyes. "Yeah, well, at least you know what you're doing with your life now. At least you *have* something to do. Other than freelance, I've got my car and what little money is in my bank account. Seems kind of pathetic."

"No," he said quietly. "Not pathetic. Like I said, brave."

His dark eyes held hers for a long moment, his quiet voice seeming to linger in the space between them. When he leaned forward to meet her lips, it seemed inevitable, natural. It wasn't even desire she felt, but affection and gratitude and—okay, the fact that this scenario had run through her mind once or twice as she was falling asleep last night. When she didn't pull away, he reached out and gripped her arm gently, his lips moving softly over hers.

And then, as if he realized what he was doing, he jerked back. "I'm sorry. I . . . don't want you to think that was planned. That's not why I brought you up here."

She resisted the impulse to feel hurt, because she could already see the conflict on his face. *First kiss since his wife and it's with a stranger. Got it.* So she just smiled at him, despite the slight ache that had formed at the gentle rejection. "It's okay. I know you didn't." She glanced at her mostly clean plate and then at the hot spring pool. "Can we put our feet in?"

"Of course we can." He stood abruptly, brushing off his jeans unnecessarily, and toed off his shoes. "It's too bad we didn't bring bathing suits . . . though let's face it, this place has seen a lot fewer bathing suits than you'd think."

Mallory laughed. "The kids come here to skinny dip?"

He smiled. "Not officially, of course."

She grinned. If it were nighttime, she might be tempted to try it, or at least tempted to strip down to her conservative sports bra and underwear. But it was brightly lit mid-day with a stranger she'd just kissed, so there was no way she was showing off anything but her feet. She unbuckled her sandals and gingerly followed him across the rocky ground to the edge of the pool.

The water was comfortably warm when she lowered herself onto a boulder near the edge of the pool and dipped her feet in. Thomas hesitated for a moment, and then took a spot on a smaller rock a couple of feet away. No doubt already regretting the kiss. She kicked her feet in the water a bit, trying not to feel hurt by the clear message, and looked around the clearing again. "Thanks for bringing me here. I'm not going to write about this part."

He blinked at her. "No?"

"No. But if you'll show me the other ones on the map, I'll write about those." She threw him a smile. "I can't ruin this for the town by telling visitors where it is. Not many places have their very own secret hot springs."

"Ah, but how would we know if they did?" he said, the twinkle back in his eye. "Maybe all these towns have their very own hot springs and they're just keeping them secret too."

She laughed. "I'll give you that one."

After they'd dangled their feet in the water for a couple of minutes, Mallory drew hers up and let them dry in the sunshine before she slipped on her shoes again. Thomas did the same, and she joined him in packing up the remnants of the picnic basket, then helped him fold up the blanket.

Before they started back to the car, she stopped and placed a light hand on his arm. "Thanks," she said sincerely. "For all of this."

He met her eyes and smiled. "Think nothing of it. It's my pleasure."

And they started back down the path in comfortable silence.

CHAPTER TEN

HE SHOULDN'T HAVE KISSED HER.

The thought chased around and around his head as they hiked back to his vehicle in silence, needling him with every step. He'd known that it would be weird for him the first time he kissed a woman who wasn't Estella, but he'd thought it would be his own reticence, his own memories that would get in the way.

Not that he would feel like he was taking advantage of a situation.

And if he were being truthful with himself, that was exactly what he had done. Mallory was clearly just out of a bad relationship—by weeks, if not by days—so much so that she'd had to flee the town where they'd lived together. And now she was essentially dependent on him for transportation and shelter, with her car in the shop and no other options for accommodations.

It made him feel like a heel. After all, she didn't know him. For all she knew, if she rejected his advances, he would kick her out of the apartment and she'd be sleeping in a doorway until her car was fixed.

She couldn't know that the people of Haven Ridge

would surely come to her rescue should that happen—
at least he hoped they would. Nor could she know just
how much they were banking on her article to do ...
something ... for the state of their beloved town.

So yeah, he shouldn't have kissed her. Even if he
couldn't exactly bring himself to regret it.

Once they loaded up the car, he drove back out to
the highway and turned west toward where the better-
known pools were located. "They call these the Three
Sisters," he said, "because—"

"There are three of them?" she guessed with a
mischievous smile. Apparently she wasn't holding the
ill-advised kiss against him.

"Wow, you're good at this," he shot back with a grin.
"And before you ask, no, I don't know where the name
came from. I mean, they're all roughly the same shape
and size, so maybe the person thought 'The Triplets'
wasn't a poetic enough name."

A few minutes later, he pulled into a paved parking
lot, which had a single car parked there, a kayak
strapped to the roof. These springs, at least, had been
conceived of as a destination—there was still the same
wild high desert foliage, but someone had erected
shade shelters with picnic tables some way down the
path.

"Don't get me wrong," Mallory said as she opened
the door, "but I like the other one better."

"Yeah, me too. Why do you think we always used to
go to that one?"

"Less likely to get caught?"

He laughed.

They hiked down the short, level path to where the
first of the pools was located, nestled beneath a rocky
outcropping dotted with native grasses. This time
Mallory pulled out her cell phone and snapped several

photos. "I'm really not sure if these are going to be usable, but I'll submit them anyway."

The next two pools were a little farther down the path and were close enough to each other that bathers could reach across the space between them and link hands. One of them was occupied by a young couple, wrapped in each other's arms, kissing. Making out, really. Thomas felt his face heat again when they looked up, and he gave an apologetic wave. "Sorry."

They broke apart, apparently as embarrassed as he felt. Mallory grabbed Thomas's hand and practically dragged him back down the path toward the parking lot. As soon as they were out of earshot, they both broke into laughter.

"I feel like a kid who walked in on her parents," she admitted.

"I think they were wearing bathing suits," he said, "but I didn't want to look close enough to know for sure."

She giggled and met his eye and they both dissolved into laughter again. They might both be grown, neither of them naive, but there was something about the situation that made him feel like a teenager again. From the color high on Mallory's cheekbones, she seemed to feel the same way.

"I kind of wanted to get a photo of the other pools," she admitted, "but that would be even weirder than what we actually did."

"Weirder than us kissing?" he asked, confused.

"No! Weirder than us running away!" She laughed, but when she stole a look at him, her expression was vulnerable. "I didn't think kissing you was weird."

He stopped. "No. Me neither."

"Then why did you apologize?"

"I didn't want you to think that I was taking advantage of the situation. It's not like you have any

options right now with your car in the shop. I didn't
want to put you in a situation where you thought you
couldn't say no."

"That's really sweet," she said, a tinge of surprise in
her voice.

"Yeah, well ... " He wasn't sure what to say again, the
shyness that he thought he'd lost until he met Mallory
Adams coming back full force.

She smiled and rose up on her tiptoes to press a soft
kiss against his lips, so quick that she was already
stepping away before he registered what happened.
"Apology accepted."

They started walking again and he debated whether
to take her hand for so long that they were back at the
SUV without him ever having made the move. Which
was probably better. Because once he eliminated the
whole issue of pressing his advantage while she had no
other options, what did he really think he was doing
anyway? Even as a college student, he hadn't been into
one-night stands. She was leaving as soon as her story
was done. So what other options were there really?

As soon as they were back in the car, she turned to
him. "I was wondering. Are there any documents that
back up the Haven Ridge history that Granny Pearl told
me? I probably should have some sort of verifiable
sources before I submit this."

"Well, there's the Chaffee County Historical Society
Museum in Buena Vista. And then there's the visitors
bureau, but to my knowledge that's sort of a ... virtual
organization."

She nodded, thinking. "I'll call or email everyone
when we get back and see what I can find out."

He backed out of the parking spot, daring a quick
look at her before he shifted into drive again. "What if
you can't find anything?"

"I'm not sure," she admitted. "Bea—my editor—is kind of a stickler for accuracy. She came from the newspaper side, where everything has to be backed up by reliable sources."

"Understandable," Thomas said, but his stomach was already sinking. He knew how difficult it was to find actual published information on the town, because when he'd done his town history project in high school, his teachers had pressed him for a more accurate bibliography than *my grandmother told me this.* Other than a few passing mentions about Haven Ridge in books about the Colorado gold rush, where it was grouped together with Salida and Granite and Buena Vista without further elaboration, there was practically nothing.

He could feel this second chance slipping away.

He was wracking his brain for something else that he could show her that would make for a good article when his phone rang. *Dean Maciolek* flashed onto the screen. Thomas answered and punched the speaker button so Mallory could hear. "Hey, Dean. I've got Mallory here with me."

"Hi, Mallory." The mechanic's voice came out tinny and distant. "I've been through your car with a fine-tooth comb and I have to say, I'm baffled."

Mallory shot Thomas a concerned look before turning her attention to the phone. "I take it you have no idea why it won't start?"

Dean paused for a long moment. "Well, that's the thing. It starts just fine. I've kept it all day, started it numerous times. I've tested the battery, alternator, and starter. All good. In fact, if I hadn't witnessed it myself, I would doubt you were having any troubles in the first place."

The pronouncement made Thomas feel a little displaced, even light-headed. "So she's good then?"

"As far as I can tell. I'm afraid I don't know what to tell you. I'll drop the car off at the cafe in a little bit. I'm sorry I can't give you any better explanation."

"Thanks, Dean. We really appreciate it." He disconnected the call and tucked the phone into the console.

"That's strange," Mallory said finally.

"Yeah. It is." If he believed Pearl, the town had fabricated a car problem to keep her here. Even if he did believe it, that meant that Mallory had seen whatever she was meant to see, and now it was time for her to move on. Good news for her, he supposed. If she wanted to, she could still go on to Salida and write her original article as planned.

But it didn't explain why he suddenly felt so disappointed.

CHAPTER ELEVEN

MALLORY HAD KISSED a virtual stranger. Twice.

The thought kept spinning around her head the short drive back to town as she waited for regret to slide in. Not that she technically had any reason *not* to kiss a handsome stranger to whom she was attracted—and who, it seemed like, was attracted to her. She no longer had a boyfriend, thanks to John's betrayal. It was just that she had been part of a couple for so long that she'd forgotten what it was like to get to know a new person, to feel out whether or not there was something worth pursuing. And of course, getting that all-important first kiss out of the way, when you determined whether those butterflies in your stomach were really interest or just a reaction to something you ate.

But there were no worries on that account. Their first kiss, soft and sweet and gentle, had nonetheless been assured and confident, a promise of what might lie ahead should she pursue it. And as she replayed it in her mind, the feel of his lips on hers, the light touch of his fingertips warming her skin, she *wanted* to pursue it.

What was she thinking, though? Not only was he a stranger, he was a stranger in a town in the middle of nowhere, a place she would be leaving in less than a day. No matter what might have sparked between them, it had absolutely no future. She was leaving. End of story. If she was smart, she would put an end to this right now, before either of them started to have any sort of crazy thoughts about the future. But even *thinking* that felt presumptuous. He'd gotten carried away and kissed her. Just because she was a serial monogamist who didn't kiss a guy unless she was thinking of long-term prospects didn't mean he had anything more in mind.

So get a grip, get your car, and get out of here before your confused, broken little heart can shatter any more than it already has this month.

Fortunately, Thomas seemed as lost in thought on the drive back as she was, so he didn't question her silence or push her for her thoughts. When he parked the SUV behind the cafe again, Mallory blurted, "I thought I might take a shower before I start packing up again. Would that be all right with you?"

He turned to her and blinked as if he'd forgotten she was even there. "Of course. Make yourself at home. There are towels in the cabinet. Feel free to use anything you find under the counter."

Mallory nodded and reached for the door handle. Then she changed her mind and fell back against the seat. "Thank you, Thomas. For showing me around today. It's a beautiful town." She wanted to say it was heartbreaking, what it had become, but how did you say something like that without sounding like a jerk?

But he seemed to understand, because he gave her a twist of a smile. "Thank you. Do you have what you need?"

"I hope so," she said. "We'll see. Even if I don't,

maybe I can do a feature for the online arm of the magazine—"

He touched her arm gently. "It's okay, Mallory. Do what you have to do. We'll be fine either way. We always are."

Mallory smiled, and this time, she did manage to get out of the car. He followed her in, waiting until she started to climb the stairs to the apartments before he continued down the hall into the restaurant. She ducked into her apartment just long enough to get her toiletry bag, then descended the stairs back down to Thomas's space.

True to his word, he'd left the door unlocked for her—but then, what was there really to guard against here? Virtually everyone knew everyone else, and it would take some real gall or desperation to steal from a neighbor. Still, she felt like she was encroaching as she pushed the door open and crept inside, then clicked the door softly shut behind her.

She stood there for a second, taking it in. She'd expected it to be a duplicate of her own, but while hers was a one-bedroom with a small parlor, this was a large studio. The open space on the left ran from the door to the back wall, the front part decorated with simple, modern furniture—not the ornate antiques that characterized Mallory's—and the back part was set up as a bedroom. To the right was an open kitchen, and she assumed the door in the back led to the bathroom. She glanced around the whole space, curious, and realized that the top two floors must once have been used as a single residence: public spaces here and private spaces upstairs. Now her cramped, closed-off kitchen made sense. It had probably once been a bedroom.

Still, it made this space feel even more intimate and her presence more of an invasion, even considering that there was virtually no sign of the man who lived here. The apartment was neat as a pin: no books sitting on the side table, no dishes in the sink. Either he was a neat freak or he really hadn't brought much back with him from Texas.

Slowly, she moved toward the back where she presumed the bathroom to be, glancing at the neatly-made bed—complete with a very bachelor-looking gray microfiber duvet—and went for the nearest door. When she opened it, though, it was not the bathroom she was looking at, but a small storage nook. Mallory began to close it until the items inside caught her eye: canvases, dozens of them.

She looked around guiltily. She knew she should walk away and let it be. This was Thomas's private space and the loan of a shower didn't give her permission to paw through his personal items. But now that she was here, she couldn't tear herself away. She had to know.

Mallory tipped the closest canvas toward herself and drew in her breath at the first glimpse. Her scruples over snooping vanished as she lifted it out and set it against the door. It was a breathtaking painting, done in hundreds of thousands of tiny dots in brilliant colors, swirls and groupings that gave it the look of mosaic performed in paint. *Pointillism*, a distant memory from undergrad art history supplied, but she hadn't remembered ever studying anything this ... alive.

She stepped back to get the full effect and realized it was a landscape, rolling hills with a brilliant sunset, rendered in bright shades that evoked a feeling rather than reproduced reality. She'd never really been able to articulate what made a painting good or bad, but she knew just by the feeling that bloomed in her chest when she looked at it that this was exceptional.

Emboldened by the discovery, she began to look at the other canvases in the closet. There were seascapes, mountains, and a cityscape or two—European, so perhaps Belgium as he'd mentioned?—all done in those brilliant shades that were too vibrant to be faithful reproductions of nature. They represented feelings, she realized, how he viewed his subject, and not just what he saw.

And then she got to the last one, facing the wood-paneled back of the closet, and sucked in a breath. Unlike the others, this was a portrait. And unlike the others, this wasn't done in bright colors, but rather tender shades of peach and gray and brown. Sunrise colors, creating the head and shoulders of a beautiful woman.

His wife, Estella. It had to be.

She stared at it for a long moment, struck by how Thomas had somehow captured emotion just through the application of tiny dots of paints, so individual and strictly demarcated, but combining into sweeps and waves of color. *Love*, she thought. He had loved Estella more than anything. And now he had this painting in the closet, facing the wall, where he couldn't be reminded of what he had lost. Of all he had lost.

Feeling suddenly melancholy, she carefully replaced all the paintings as she'd found them and shut the door. He was just as hurt by his past experiences as she was. He had lost his footing, his foundation, just as surely as she had. Their kiss had been one brief moment of commonality, commiseration, but it didn't mean anything. Not when he hid his art in a literal closet, shutting himself off from the things he had loved.

Mallory moved into the bathroom through the other door, barely noting the gleaming white subway tiles and the old-fashioned claw-foot tub. Instead, she turned on the faucet in the small, stand-up shower behind its glass door, retrieved a fluffy white towel from the antique cabinet in the corner, and hung her toiletry bag on the hook on the wall. She scrubbed her body with her bar of scented soap, washed her hair, and then toweled off again, all automatically. She couldn't explain the strange feelings that were coursing through her body. Disappointment, for certain. Sadness, too, but whether it was for herself or for Thomas and all that he had lost, she wasn't sure. And then, beneath it all, a tiny flicker of determination.

She couldn't be sad for Thomas's talent locked away in the closet, untouched and unused, without recognizing the parallels. She had once had a passion, something that had driven her to scrimp and save and work so she could get her degree, so she could research the history of people and places that had been forgotten. In her desperation to feel like she belonged—to someone, in this case—she'd given it all up. She'd allowed herself to be made small, to be put in a box, to believe that what she wanted wasn't as important as what John wanted, that she didn't deserve to pursue her own goals. And even though she was, in a small sense, using that passion in what she was doing now, she was no different than Thomas, locking the parts of herself that made her special and enthusiastic and ... a person ... in a symbolic closet.

That flicker stoked into a flame, warming her from the inside out, building excitement in her body. She pulled her clothes on hastily, hopping around the tile floor as she got her jeans stuck on her damp feet, then combed out her hair and twisted it on top of her head without heeding the wet drips that it left down the back of her shirt. Maybe she had been brought here for a reason. Maybe it wasn't so much that the town needed her story, but that she needed the town and *its* story to remind her of what she loved most. About who she'd been before she decided she had to sacrifice everything to be loved.

She gathered her things, wiped down the shower and the sink, and then returned upstairs to her borrowed apartment, where she set up her laptop and notebooks on the parlor table in the living area. Then she grabbed her cell phone, typed *Haven Ridge Chaffee County historical society* into the browser, and began making calls.

CHAPTER TWELVE

THOMAS HAD BARELY GOTTEN BACK into the cafe and taken his place behind the counter when Granny Pearl walked in, locked onto him like a heat-seeking missile. Today she was wearing another one of her Oxfords—this one blue and embroidered with pink flamingos—with a pair of pink skinny jeans and white high-tops. She slid onto the stool and fixed him with her no-nonsense stare. "So?"

He wasn't going to make this easy on her. "So, what?"

"You know what I mean, young man. Did you do it? Did you convince Mallory?"

He threw her a slight smile. "I don't know if I convinced her, but she was definitely charmed by the time we were done. Loved the architecture of the town, was enchanted by the hot spring pools. I got the impression that she's going to write the article, but she was concerned her editor might need more accurate sources than just the say-so of a Haven Ridge old-timer."

Granny Pearl puffed herself up for a second before she realized he was teasing her, then shot him a mock-glare. "You need to have more respect for your elders."

"And you need to let her do what she's going to do. I'm not going to strong-arm her into writing an article if it's going to get her in trouble or lose her this gig. She needs it. She hasn't had all that much luck in her life. And I'm not going to be another person manipulating her into doing what I want against her best interests."

Now Granny's expression shifted, crafty and thoughtful. "You like her."

He didn't even try to deny it. "I do."

She looked at him more closely. "You kissed her."

He blinked at her, genuinely shocked. "How could you possibly know that?"

"Because you just told me, boy." She grinned, pleased with herself.

Thomas sighed and rolled his eyes, swiveling away for a mug and the coffee pot. He poured his grandmother a cup of coffee. "What are you really doing here?"

"Just checking." She looked at him closely. "Just making sure everything is as it's supposed to be."

"I told you, I have no control over what she's writing. She seemed charmed by the town, amazed that it was dwindling, legitimately thought the story of its origin would make a good article."

"I'm not talking about her, I'm talking about you."

He frowned at his grandmother, and she softened, reaching across the counter to place her hand on his wrist.

"You've been carrying around this grief for so long. When Mallory Adams walked into our town—into your life—for the first time in years, I saw a spark of that boy I remembered. Estella wouldn't want you to grieve her forever. She would want you to be happy." She paused and fixed him with a significant look. "You know, she talked to me on that last trip you made back here."

Thomas stiffened. Despite her teasing, Estella had loved Haven Ridge as much as he did, and in the last six months of her life, she'd insisted on going back for what would turn out to be one last trip. They'd stayed in the apartment upstairs, the one that Mallory now occupied, but he hadn't realized that she and his grandmother had had any time to talk alone.

He cleared his throat. "What did you talk about, exactly?"

Pearl regarded him with a sad smile. "She was worried about you. She felt guilty about marrying you, like she entrapped you. Even though she hadn't known about the cancer, she felt like she had stolen your chance for a real life, for a happily-ever-after. And she made me promise that when you were ready, I would tell you."

Thomas blinked back the first prick of tears. "Tell me what?"

"That it was okay to move on. That she wanted you to be happy. That she hoped you would fall in love again."

He took a long shaky breath. It sounded like Estella, but the fact that she'd been looking out for him long before she died, knowing how he would hold onto her memory even though they had only known each other for three short years ... He refocused on the last part of the statement. "I'm not in love, Granny."

"Not yet. But you will be, someday. And she wanted you to know that you had her blessing."

Thomas stared down at the countertop for a moment. It was a lot to take in. And yet ...

"Thank you," he said. "I think I needed to hear that."

"I know you did." Pearl patted his hand reassuringly. "I'm going home now. I'm old. I'll see you later."

Thomas watched his grandmother go, unsure of how he felt right now. He'd meant what he said. He'd known

Mallory for twenty-four hours, so there was no way he was in love with her. He didn't know her at all. But he liked her. Something about her called to him, made him want to know more. And thanks to his grandmother and his late wife, he didn't have to feel guilty about it.

For the first time in three years, his life felt like it belonged to him again and not his grief.

For the first time in three years, he thought he was finally ready to move on.

* * *

Thomas waited for Mallory to come down to the cafe for dinner, but as the night stretched and she didn't appear, he began to wonder if she'd had second thoughts about what had happened between them that day. They were both adults and it had only been a kiss, but maybe she'd realized that it had been a mistake given that she would be moving on as soon as her article was finished.

Never mind the fact that since his conversation with Granny earlier today, he was beginning to wish more and more that she didn't have to leave.

As the clock crept toward closing time, he decided to be proactive and placed two orders with the kitchen. Then as soon as he locked the doors and flipped the sign, he took the foil to-go containers up two flights of stairs and rapped on her door.

"Come in," she called absently.

He turned the knob and nudged the door open, shutting it behind him with his elbow. Mallory sat in the middle of the parlor in the dark apartment, staring at the glowing screen of her laptop. She barely looked up when he walked in.

"I thought you might be hungry so I brought you something before the kitchen closed."

That got through her daze. She blinked as if she hadn't realized that time had passed, that night had fallen around her, and shoved the laptop onto the parlor table. "What time is it?" she asked, blinking owlishly.

He flipped the switch near the door, flooding the room with light. "A little after eight." He brought the containers over to the table. "I hope you don't mind company. I didn't have time to eat tonight." Not exactly the truth ... he'd kept himself busy with other things waiting for her so they'd have the opportunity to eat together. It was just luck that they got to do it in private and not downstairs under the watchful eyes of the town grapevine.

"No, I don't mind at all. I meant to come down earlier, I just got caught up in what I was doing."

Thomas moved into the kitchen, flipping on the light there, too, and coming back out with two stoneware plates and a handful of silverware. "I hope you like meatloaf."

Mallory grimaced.

"You don't? This might change your mind. This is Granny Pearl's recipe, and it's been known to make believers out of doubters for almost seventy years."

She chuckled. "With that kind of endorsement, I have to give it a try."

He wasn't lying. Granny's meatloaf was a Haven Ridge institution and the most beloved thing on his grandfather's menu; he'd had to beg her to give Arnold the recipe, and in the end, she'd made Arnold sign an NDA before she handed it over. Even now, the thought made him laugh. He opened the foil containers, portioned out the food in the most artistic arrangement he could manage, and then handed it over to Mallory. She took it, her expression still doubtful.

Until she took a bite. "This is delicious!" she exclaimed around a mouthful of food.

"I know." Thomas grinned at her. "I told you."

She devoured half the food in silence—the mashed potatoes were almost as good as the meatloaf itself, in Thomas's opinion—while he ate more slowly, watching her. After a little time had passed, he asked casually, "So how is the article going?"

"Good. I'm waiting to hear back from someone at UCCS. I followed down a lead from the various local historical societies and found a professor in the history department who specializes in this region and time period. He was in his office when I called, so he said he would track down some information and send it over tomorrow or Monday. Assuming it all checks out, I can finish my article and send it on to my editor."

"Wow, that's great," he said, though inwardly his heart was already falling. If she was that close to being done, that meant she was moving on. "What are you going to do now?"

"I don't know," she said finally. "But I had a realization today."

"Oh?"

"I want to go back to school and finish my master's degree."

Thomas blinked. That was not what he'd expected. "That's great. Where?"

"I don't know yet. I think if I move back to Seattle, I can probably just resume my studies at UW. It was only my seminar paper that I needed to finish. I already had the rest of my graduate credits."

"So that's what? Another year?"

"For the master's, yes. But it's not a terminal degree. You're expected to continue on to a Ph.D. So really, it's another four years."

"I see," Thomas said softly. "Well, congratulations. That's a big decision."

It was unreasonable to feel disappointed. She was never going to stay, hadn't intended to in the first place. But somewhere deep down, he'd hoped that maybe he and Haven Ridge had made enough of an impression on her to change her plans. Even to come back once she'd gone away. But if she had already decided to move back to Washington, to resume her life at the point it had been interrupted by a man who hadn't respected her wishes or her dreams, Thomas wasn't going to be the one who tried to talk her out of that. She'd had enough of people trying to bend her to their own wishes. But despite his attempt to be supportive, his words must not have rung entirely true.

"It is a big decision," she said softly, looking at him closely. "You don't think it's the right one?"

"It doesn't matter what I think. It only matters what you think. If that's your dream, if that's what you've always wanted to do, you should pursue it."

She nodded slowly, her eyes lingering on him, then went back to the remnants of her meal. He watched her for a second, then realized what he'd forgotten to mention. He took a set of keys from his pocket and placed them on the table. "Your car is back. Dean drove it over this evening."

"Oh," she said. "Thank you. What do I owe him?"

"Nothing. He said to tell you if you run into problems after you leave, call him for another tow."

"That's nice of him."

"I think he feels a little guilty he didn't find something. He's not just the only mechanic in town. He really is the best."

Mallory pushed up from the sofa and held her hand out for his plate. He handed it over and followed her to the kitchen, where she scraped the remnants into a trash can and began washing the dishes. "I guess I'll be going in the morning, then," she said carefully, setting first one dish, then the other into the dish drainer on the counter. "I finished a draft of the article tonight, but just in case, I thought maybe I'd run over to Salida and catch the last day of the whitewater festival."

"That sounds like a plan."

She must have picked up something in his voice, because she stilled, the water running into the sink the only sound in the quiet. He reached past her and shut off the faucet, his chest pressing against her shoulder, his arm brushing hers.

She didn't move, but he felt the sudden acceleration of her breathing and took his time drawing back. She slowly turned and leaned back against the counter, raising those wide green eyes to his while her lips parted in invitation. The moment stretched between them, crackling with electricity like an impending lightning strike.

This time when their lips met, it was neither gentle nor restrained. Her arms slid around his waist, her fingernails raking up his back as she pulled him closer, making his head swim and his body throb with sudden, uncontrolled desire. He pulled the clip out of her hair and tossed it away, burying his fingertips into the damp strands. She moaned as his lips left hers to travel across the soft skin of her jaw and her neck before returning to devour her mouth once more.

"Thomas," she whispered, fisting her hands in his shirt to pull him even closer. Her lips sought his again, but it was that single word that brought him crashing back to reality.

What was he doing? He had to be crazy. She was leaving tomorrow, moving on with her dream—over a thousand miles away. If this went any further, there was no way it could turn out well for either of them. They would be left with nothing but regret.

Or maybe she wouldn't regret it. Maybe she just wanted to wipe away the memory of her ex. But he knew for certain that once he started thinking of her as his, he would never want to let her go.

Even as he marveled that he could still think so rationally, he gripped her shoulders and took a big step back. "I'm sorry."

She stared up at him, eyes wide, but there was a flicker of anger in her expression. "Don't you dare tell me that you didn't mean to do that."

"No. I meant every bit of that." His gaze roamed her face, taking in her flushed cheeks and kiss-bruised lips, and a fist wrapped around his heart. He brushed an errant strand of hair from her cheek and tucked it behind her ear. "Which is why I'm going to go now. I wish you all success, Mallory. In everything."

And then he turned on his heel and left.

CHAPTER THIRTEEN

MALLORY DIDN'T SLEEP THAT NIGHT, tossing and turning in the soft bed of her temporary shelter. It wasn't just the memory of Thomas's kiss, though replaying it over and over in her mind certainly didn't do anything but make her frustrated and regretful that he'd come to his senses, even while she was grateful that he had. She was leaving tomorrow, and it was unlikely that she would ever come back to Haven Ridge. This had been an accident, a detour. A distraction.

Because what was there here for her, really? The fact that she was wishing that she didn't have to go had far more to do with a handsome guy who had made her feel special after she'd had her heart broken than any real belief that she belonged in this town. Even if her article was approved, even if she did have the sources to back it up, it probably wouldn't do a single thing for the town's slow decline. Sometimes small towns just died. However charming and historical and filled with good people they might be.

Because she did believe that it was filled with good people. Thomas and Granny Pearl and Dean Maciolek had treated her not as a stranded traveler but a friend. And while she could certainly argue that they were doing it because they wanted something out of her, she didn't believe it. She knew when she was being used, however laughable that might seem after her experience with John.

But somewhere inside her she'd known she was being used there, too, that she was just an accessory to his life and not something essential to it. As soon as he'd found someone better, he'd moved on.

She had a feeling that Thomas would never do anything like that. Besides, Granny Pearl would murder him if he tried.

Mallory smiled at that thought, imagining what it would be like to walk with Thomas through town hand-in-hand, greeted as if she belonged there. To actually feel like part of a community.

To feel like part of a family.

And just as quickly as she'd allowed herself to indulge that fantasy, she shut it down. Because that's all that it was. A fantasy. She was conflating a few kisses and one nice day with dreams for the future, and wasn't that always what she did?

Besides, she'd meant what she'd said to Thomas about going back to school. It was time for her to reclaim her life and the goals she had given up. Clearly the easiest way to do that was to return to Washington and finish the degree she'd started. Build a life based on what *she* wanted, not what everyone else around her wanted. Not based on what a man told her she should do.

Except classes won't begin until September, a voice whispered in her head. *It's only June. You don't have a place to live. Why couldn't you just stay here in Haven Ridge until it's time to go?*

"Because there's no work for me here," she said aloud in the dark, arguing against that hopeful internal voice. "And because ... "

And because I'm afraid. I'm afraid to want something so badly and not get it. Like always.

She rolled to her back and stared at the ceiling, the rosettes and crown moldings cast into relief by the little bit of light that seeped between the curtains from the street below. If she left now, she could believe that Haven Ridge was everything she wanted and hoped it could be. It could remain an idyllic town in her memory, struggling but filled with kind-hearted people. It could validate her belief that good people and places could still exist, that people could care for a stranger and welcome her into their community. And as long as she left before she was proved wrong, she could hold onto that hope.

And what good is hope for a place to belong if you're never going to take a risk and grab it for yourself?

Her inner voice was annoying. Because it was 100% right.

She smashed a pillow over her face to muffle her groan. This was stupid. She had to leave. People didn't break down in a town and just decide to make a home there with no way to support themselves. At least not in real life.

What Haven Ridge wants, Haven Ridge gets. Granny Pearl's words came back to Mallory, not ominous but promising. What if there really was something to her theory of the town? After all, there had been nothing wrong with her car that anyone could find. And in all the years she'd used her GPS it had never taken her to a totally different place than her intended destination. It was like the hand of something or someone had reached down and decided she was supposed to be here at this time for some as-yet-unnamed purpose.

A wild thought gripped her, no doubt a product of her lack of sleep and the mad sensibilities of the midnight hours. If this town had really brought her here, she'd let it decide.

"Fine," she said aloud, speaking to the air around her and feeling foolish even as she did. "If you want me here for some reason, you're going to have to give me a sign. If Haven Ridge is all it claims to be, if there's something to Elizabeth Strong's visions and this so-called purpose of the town, prove it. And then maybe I'll stay."

She listened but heard nothing in the dark except the creaks of an old building and the soft chirp of crickets outside her window. She rolled her eyes at her own stupidity and burrowed under the covers again. But sleep was a long time in coming.

Because no matter how hard she tried to protect herself from reality, she wanted to believe.

* * *

Knowing Mallory was ten feet above him and it might as well be a mile was absolute torture.

Thomas sat up in his bed, a book propped on his chest within the glow of his bedside lamp, but he didn't truly see the words. He'd done everything that Pearl had asked of him. He'd showed Mallory the town and he'd thought she was finally understanding what would make him come back here after so many years away. She had written the article, but he knew she still didn't *believe*. If she couldn't corroborate Pearl's stories, this whole thing had been a waste. There would be no needed boost for the town and she would move on to her next assignment.

Leaving him here thinking about a woman that he couldn't have. The first woman since Estella died who made him wonder what life could be like if he were to put aside his grief and move on.

Thomas shut the book with more force than necessary and shoved it aside. He was being stupid. He actually had convinced himself that he was falling for a stranger, simply because she was the first woman he'd kissed since his wife.

And yet . . .

It wasn't mere lust or attraction. He liked her. More than that, he felt a connection to her. He felt comfortable with her. He'd never been particularly outgoing; Estella had been the one who had organized the outings and the parties and convinced him that he needed more in his life than just her and work and painting. He could talk about art for hours, which was why he'd loved his job, but he'd always been happier alone with his thoughts and his imagination than with other people. Except for Estella, who felt like she was his other half. People might assume he was extroverted because he ran the Brick House Cafe, but that was just because Haven Ridge was his family. He didn't have to hide or pretend with them. He'd grown up here, he belonged here. He was always going to belong here, no matter how long he left or how far he roamed.

And yet he'd taken an instant liking to Mallory. Being with her was easy. Felt right. Even his initial attempts to keep his distance had only been because he was denying that there was another person with whom he could instantly click. He'd always told himself that the minute he'd seen Estella, he'd known she was his soulmate.

What did that mean if he felt the same way about someone else three short years after she died? Didn't that somehow diminish what he'd had with his wife? Didn't that mean he'd been deluding himself about the idea that they'd been meant to be together if it had taken him so little time to feel that same, instantaneous connection with someone else?

Didn't that mean he was somehow betraying her memory?

But Estella had known he would feel that way or she wouldn't have talked to Pearl when they came for their last visit. She'd known that left to his own devices, he would stay lonely and single forever, pining for her and using his pain and misery to fuel his art. Except he hadn't even done that, all his supplies packed away, his paintings shoved in a closet where he didn't have to look at them and understand everything he'd lost. She would be disappointed in him. If she were looking down on him now, she was probably shaking her head with that amused, exasperated smile and saying, "Stop being an idiot, Thomas. Stop overthinking things. Just be happy."

And somewhere, deep inside him, he thought that maybe Mallory would make him happy.

Not that that was her responsibility. He knew that. But loving her—someday, if she'd let him—would fill the parts of his heart that had been cracked and broken. Maybe. Possibly. If she weren't leaving tomorrow to go back to Washington and follow the dreams that had been interrupted.

He shook his head. He couldn't do that to her. He couldn't even bring up the idea of her staying, not after what had happened with her ex. She'd given up everything for a guy who didn't respect her, didn't love her, didn't care about her. And while Thomas knew he wasn't that sort of man, if he asked her to do the same thing, he might as well be. Because loving someone— even loving the *idea* of them—meant doing what was best for them. Even if it wasn't best for himself.

Maybe that was the whole point of this exercise. Maybe it wasn't that he and Mallory were supposed to be together. If there was any special magic to Haven Ridge, it was that it took people who were broken and betrayed and put them on the right path. For her, maybe that was making her realize that she could go back, finish what she'd started, erase the detour that had taken her so far away from her goals. For him, it might simply have been to open his eyes and heart to the possibility of moving on. Loving again. Letting go of the grief as Estella had wanted him to do.

And while that wasn't what he *wanted*, maybe that was exactly what they needed.

CHAPTER FOURTEEN

MALLORY AWOKE JUST AFTER EIGHT, groggy and with her head pounding. She had no idea when she'd finally fallen asleep, just that it must have been close to dawn because the light coming in through the crack in the curtains had a distinctly blue cast. She groaned as she threw back the covers and fumbled for her suitcase to find leggings and a sweatshirt for the drive to Salida. What she really wanted was a long, hot shower to transform her from the walking dead into a coherent human, but there was no way she was going to go downstairs and invade Thomas's privacy again.

She settled for a splash of ice-cold water in the sink, carefully brushed her hair into a neat bun, and swiped on a coat of mascara and lip gloss—as much of an effort as she could bring herself to make this morning. She was leaving. She would probably never see anyone here again. Why should she make an effort?

Her middle-of-the-night plea to Haven Ridge now felt fanciful and foolish—as if a town could actually do anything, as if there was anything more to Pearl's story than family legends and wishful thinking. And yet there was a tiny kernel of hope inside as she packed up her things and straightened the apartment. She wanted to believe that there was more to life than just the consequences of her own stupid decisions, that there was someone out there who was looking out for her. That she had been brought here for a reason beyond a simple software glitch.

And even if she was going to be disappointed in the end, at least for the next few hours, she could live in that little bubble of hope.

Once she was satisfied that the apartment was clean, she extended the handle on her suitcase and rolled it out onto the landing. The smells of breakfast and the clank of silverware told her that the cafe was in full swing this morning, and her heart lifted at the prospect of seeing Thomas behind the counter, waiting for her with that wry smile, the warmth in his brown eyes.

And yet when she bumped the suitcase down the two long flights of stairs and rolled it toward the counter at the front of the restaurant, the person standing there was not Thomas, but Madeline. She looked up when Mallory approached and flashed her a bright smile. "Good morning! Can I get you something to eat?"

Mallory tried to speak, but all that came out was a tired croak. She cleared her throat and tried again. "Where's Thomas?"

"I don't know," the girl said. "He texted me early this morning and asked if I could work today." She looked awfully chipper for a teenage girl who had been called into the restaurant at dawn, but maybe she was just happy for the extra hours. Mallory had always been glad for every dollar that she could earn in high school.

She slid onto a stool and drew the suitcase up beside her. "Can we start with coffee? Black?"

"Coming right up." Madeline swiveled away for the coffee pot and mug, filled it in front of her, and then left her with one of the laminated menus. Mallory scanned it without seeing what it said. Where could Thomas be? Had he regretted kissing her so much last night that he couldn't face her today? His last words to her had certainly sounded like a farewell, but she hadn't actually thought that was the last time she'd see him. Her stomach clenched at the idea that she was just going to have to drive away without saying goodbye.

She mulled the idea for so long that when Madeline came back to take her order, she hadn't even looked at the menu. "Liège waffle," she said automatically, shoving the sheet back at the girl. "I should probably have one last one before I go."

The teen smiled noncommittally, took the menu, and swiveled back to the pass to put the order in. Mallory pulled out her phone and checked her email—nothing important—then began some mindless scrolling through social media. But that only left her feeling worse than ever—all the people who looked like they had their lives together, even if she objectively knew that social was only the highlight reel and not the reality for everyone she followed—and she shut it down. Instead, she pulled up the website for the University of Washington history department and started reading over the admission requirements.

Except that didn't really help her either because she was a special case. She suspected that not only would she have to apply again, she would have to get permission from the department to resume her studies. Not to mention the fact that a combination of scholarships and grants was the only reason she'd been able to attend in the first place. Some of those had expired the minute she turned twenty-five. Others might not apply because she'd not done her studies continuously. She would have to borrow the tuition fees and hope somehow that her eventual job would pay well enough to live on and still allow her to pay off her student loans. She'd probably have to move somewhere in the Midwest like Nebraska or Oklahoma or Kansas where rent was low and salaries were still moderate.

Her optimistic words of last night were starting to feel like a fantasy.

Or maybe that was just the result of three hours of sleep and too little caffeine. She sipped her coffee, willing it to bring optimism along with alertness. When Madeline brought her waffle a few minutes later, as golden and delicious and fragrant as it had been the first time around, she dug into it and hoped the sugar would give her a lift.

"How is it?" Madeline asked with a smile when she came by again. The girl really did have a remarkable amount of poise for a teenager.

"It's good," Mallory said automatically, but the truth was, she hadn't even tasted it. She couldn't stop thinking about Thomas and what his absence from the restaurant meant this morning.

She was just about finished with her meal when her phone chimed with an alert—email. Her heart lifted at the same time that her stomach twisted when she saw the *uccs.edu* email address. Her contact in the history department had written back to her.

Hello, Mallory. Your call yesterday had me intrigued. The story you brought me about the origin of Haven Ridge is an interesting one for sure, and one that would be groundbreaking in our understanding of the history of Chaffee County before the turn of the twentieth century. I wish I could be of more help, but I'm afraid I simply have nothing in my files that relates to the town or any of its earliest incarnations.

That's not to say that there isn't some truth to the local legends, but we simply have no evidence that the town was founded by Elizabeth Strong. In fact, the earliest known reference to Haven Ridge is in 1906 with the completion of the Larkspur House by the esteemed author Andrew Bixby. It seems more likely from my knowledge of the area that it remained a small, loosely associated community until the 1890s when the first permanent buildings were built. The extant documents suggest it was the influence of Andrew Bixby that allowed it to be incorporated into a town in 1901 as opposed to simply being regarded as part of Buena Vista.

I'm sorry I couldn't be of more help in validating the local stories of Haven Ridge, but the primary sources just aren't there at present. If you do turn up any sort of documents or photos, I'd love to be kept in the loop. This part of Colorado is my personal passion project, if you will, and it's disappointing that we still know so little.

I wish you the best with your article, and do call on me if I can be of any further assistance.

Dr. Brian Emmer

Mallory lowered the phone, her heart sinking with it. If there was anyone who would know anything about whether the Haven Ridge story was real, it would be Dr. Emmer. He'd written a book and several monographs on the area, and he was one of the primary experts on the history of this part of Colorado. If he said he hadn't found any evidence pertaining to Elizabeth Strong or Haven Ridge, that was because there was nothing to be found. Mallory knew as well as he did that proving out the stories would be revolutionary. A woman founding a town on her own? Without a man?

One that was apparently important enough to draw the attention of industrialist and later famous novelist, Andrew Bixby? Someone would have written about it already if there was anything to write about.

Which meant that the legends that Granny Pearl had told her were just that—legends. Even if Pearl got them directly from her own great-grandmother, that didn't mean they were true. The woman might have been fond of tall tales or perhaps she just edited the truth to show her family in a more favorable light. After all, women rarely succeeded in the Old West on their own, and she may have been justifying some hard decisions she'd had to make for her survival. Maybe her hatred of the vice in Salida had come from personal experience.

"You okay?" Madeline asked, pausing on one of her sweeps of the counter, looking concerned.

Mallory looked up and shoved the phone into her pocket, then forced a smile. "Sure. I think I'm done here. Would you mind getting my check and a to-go cup for my coffee?"

"Sure." The girl disappeared and returned a minute later with both the check and a Styrofoam cup filled to the brim with fresh coffee. "Here you go."

Mallory fumbled with her wallet and managed to pay the ticket without focusing on what she was doing. She found her car key in her purse and wandered out to her vehicle, sliding the cup into the holder before she levered herself into the driver's seat. Then she sat with her hand on the key in the ignition, holding her breath.

Don't start, she thought silently. *I'm not done here yet.*

The engine turned over smoothly on the first try.

Mallory sucked in a breath and blinked back tears. So that was it. It was all over. The story of Haven Ridge had only been a legend and her car trouble was just a strange glitch. As had been the GPS malfunction. She'd wanted so badly to believe in some sort of homey practical magic that for a day or two, she'd let herself be seduced by the stories. The idea that somehow she was important enough that a town—an actual town—had come alive and brought her here. That she'd belonged somewhere so strongly that fate had intervened and deposited her exactly where she needed to be. But it was all her imagination, just a quick and forgettable flight of fancy constructed out of bad luck and coincidence.

Even so, that was easier to believe than the other possibility.

That there really was some magic to Haven Ridge. That she really had been brought here for a reason. And because she had failed in her attempt to write a story about it, it had rejected her just as surely as everyone else in her life.

She slammed her gearshift into reverse and backed out of the parking space. Then she put it into drive and prepared to leave the town and its whole stupid, beautiful, false legend behind.

CHAPTER FIFTEEN

MALLORY'S LAST NIGHT IN HAVEN RIDGE was the longest night that Thomas could remember in ages. He slept in fits and starts, waking thinking that he'd missed her departure, only to fall back asleep and repeat the whole process over again. Finally, around dawn, he gave up and got out of bed, padding to the kitchen and freezing his bare feet against the cold floor to make a pot of coffee.

The whole thing was ridiculous and he knew it. There wasn't anything he could do. Her mind was already made up about her future, and whether or not she submitted the article was out of his hands. Either she would find evidence that Granny Pearl's stories about Haven Ridge were true or she wouldn't. There wasn't a whole lot he could do about it.

Or was there? He distinctly recalled flipping through old photo albums and digging through boxes of diaries and photos when he was a child, but he hadn't seen any of those as an adult. Granny Pearl had done a clean sweep of the house when his grandfather had died, not because she was trying to erase his memory but simply because he had been a pack rat who hadn't allowed her to get rid of anything while he was alive. He'd been born in the middle of the Great Depression, and he'd remembered how scarce not just food but basic supplies had been, so he was never willing to throw out anything that still had life in it. Pearl had confined his collections to the detached garage, his study, and the attic, but that had still left a massive amount of stuff to sort through after his passing.

But Thomas knew that the important things were somewhere, and he knew just where he would start. Even if it took him all morning, he would dig up something that would prove to Mallory that everything his grandmother had told her about the history of Haven Ridge was true.

He glanced at the clock—5:03—and then texted Madeline to see if she would be able to come in and cover him this morning. She was a cross-country runner, so he knew she normally woke early to train before she went to one of her several part-time jobs. Sure enough, twenty minutes later, he had her chirpy response. **Sure, see you then!**

That meant she would be there before the restaurant began seating, though Arnold would already be here opening the kitchen. Even though he could get away with doing his prep in the middle of the first few orders—they were always the same five people with the same five orders, none of which were more complicated than eggs, bacon, and toast—his long years of fine dining had established a routine that the vagaries of small-town life would never banish. But that made it easy on Thomas. He didn't even need to show up this morning.

With his mind made up, he quickly threw on a pair of jeans and a sweatshirt, then retrieved his keys from where he'd dropped them on the coffee table last night. Then he descended the stairs to the ground floor, went outside, and unlocked an unmarked steel door.

This corridor was narrow and lit with a single bare bulb, showing stairs that went straight up to the second floor. Long ago, the building had been subdivided to make a single-family home—which had been subdivided further in the 1950s to make a second apartment—with the other side of the second and third floors set aside for storage. Now it simply housed all of his grand-parents' unneeded but still valuable or sentimental items.

He climbed the stairs with alacrity, eager to dig into what he assumed would be his grandmother's neatly ordered storage. But his jaw dropped when he entered the second-floor storeroom. On the right side were a number of pieces of antique furniture—the things he'd moved out of the apartment to make room for his own furniture. Farther in were some even older pieces that must have come out of Pearl's house, though he didn't recognize them. But the left side was filled with boxes, stacked haphazardly almost to the ceiling, with no seeming regard to what might be inside them. He saw crates marked *linens* next to boxes marked *books*; some had no labels at all. He sighed and stood back to decide how he was going to tackle this disaster. If he did it logically, he could put it into some kind of order so they wouldn't have to search should they need something again.

On second thought ... he ran back downstairs, let himself into his office in the back of the restaurant, and grabbed two thick Sharpies, then returned and dug into the mess.

It was worse than he'd thought, because even the boxes that were marked didn't turn out to have the things inside that they claimed. He soon figured out that he had to open every single one, rifle through the contents to make sure it wasn't what he was looking for, and then mark the actual contents on the outside. Fortunately, the first several he tackled were obvious— what looked to be tablecloths and some nice, if old-fashioned, heavy velvet curtains. He marked those and started a textiles stack in the corner.

His heart leaped when he came across one marked *Photos,* but when he opened it, it turned out to be the contents of a desk—outdated paperwork, checkbook registers, and a solitary photo album that appeared to be from the 1970s. Potentially interesting, but not helpful in his quest. He set the album aside, intending to create a box of memorabilia, and moved on to the next.

But by the time he finished the first stack of boxes, it was already seven thirty and he hadn't come up with anything even remotely related to the town's history. Now that it was a decent hour, he pulled out his cell phone and dialed Granny Pearl.

"Didn't expect to hear from you so early," she said by way of greeting.

He didn't waste time either. "I'm looking for the old family photos. The ones from the Strong side of the family. You have any idea where they are?"

She fell silent for a moment. "I imagine they're in the storage above the restaurant."

Perfect. "Thanks. I'm there right now, I just haven't come across them yet."

"Or they could be in the attic at the house. I'm not sure where I put them. But I know I didn't throw them away. They're important historical documents, you know."

"I know," he said. "That's why I'm looking for them. For Mallory."

"Oh." Granny Pearl gave a little laugh. "Now why didn't I think of that?"

No idea, but he felt like a total idiot that it had taken the threat of Mallory leaving to think of searching. "I'll let you know what I find."

"You do that," Pearl said cheerfully. "Are you coming for dinner tonight as usual?"

"I'll be there," he said and clicked off the line. He was only halfway through the boxes, and time was ticking away.

But by the time he closed up the final box, he had to admit that he wasn't going to find the photos in this room. He'd opened each one, investigating their contents, marking them properly, and grouping them in zones so he didn't have to do this search the next time he needed something. He'd found several photo albums, but they were all more contemporary than he wanted. He'd even found one of him and his sisters as children, which he set aside to look at later. But nothing from further back than the 1940s and absolutely nothing that could prove what Granny Pearl had told Mallory about Haven Ridge was true.

He sat back on his heels and sighed. He was grimy and sweaty and now he felt like he needed a shower. He'd been hoping he could go up to Mallory's apartment and give her good news before she left, but the best he could do was promise he'd keep looking. Or maybe she'd be intrigued enough to stay another day and help him look. Her deadline was still two days away, so surely she could spare the afternoon to avoid having to write another article.

He stopped first at his own apartment to wash his hands and face, then continued up the stairs to Mallory's flat. He knocked and waited. No answer. Another knock with similar results. He carefully turned the knob and poked his head in. "Mallory? It's Thomas. Are you in here?"

When there was still no answer, he swung the door wide and stepped inside. Everything was neat, cleaner in fact than when Mallory had walked in the first time. He gingerly approached the bedroom in case she was still sleeping, but the door was wide open, showing a similarly vacated room, the bed made, towels folded neatly on the end of the bed.

She was gone.

Or at least not here. He glanced at his watch, his heart sinking when he saw it was after eleven. He'd had no idea it had gotten so late. Had he missed her? Maybe she was downstairs, eating lunch.

He closed the apartment and descended the two floors into the restaurant, silently praying he'd see Mallory sitting at the counter chatting with Madeline. But the girl was taking an order from one of the booths, and the counter was empty.

Thomas caught Madeline on her way back to the kitchen. "Hey, have you seen Mallory?"

"She stopped in for breakfast this morning before she left."

"Wait, what do you mean, she left?"

The teen stared at him like he'd suddenly become hard of hearing. "She left. She took her car and went." She gestured toward the parking spaces in front of the plate glass windows, pointing out something that Thomas should have noticed immediately.

Mallory's car was gone.

CHAPTER SIXTEEN

SALIDA WAS PACKED. Everywhere Mallory went, there were SUVs bearing kayaks or paddle boards on their roofs, pedestrians wearing outdoor clothes or walking dogs. She navigated down F Street, which was the town's main drag, until she hit roadblocks, then turned down one of the intersecting streets. After spending the weekend in Haven Ridge, it was like entering an alternate reality. The buildings were similar in style and vintage, lots of red brick, some painted in pastel colors with murals on their sides. But that was where the similarities ended. The town was bursting with life, particularly on a festival weekend, and packed with so many people that she was beginning to feel downright claustrophobic.

This is what Haven Ridge could be, if only ... Except she didn't know how to finish the sentence. She didn't know why Haven Ridge was dwindling while Salida was thriving. It couldn't simply be because of lack of press. Surely someone would have discovered the small town between two thriving communities of Salida and Buena Vista, and if the property prices here were any indication, people would be happy it existed.

Mallory finally found street parking several blocks over from Riverside Park, which was near the white-water kayak course. It seemed strange to see the river so close to the town, even though surely that was why it had been built there in the first place. She shoved her laptop into her backpack, pocketed her phone, and locked her vehicle before proceeding on foot.

There was plenty to do and see today, and Mallory wandered aimlessly, snapping pictures, making notes on the app in her phone. But her heart wasn't in it. This story was second best in her mind, a necessary evil to keep from being fired from this job. It wasn't what she wanted to write about. Salida didn't need her, didn't need any more people to know about its existence. From what she could tell, there were already too many people who knew about it—she spent more time dodging pedestrians or stepping over dog leashes than she did actually walking.

Or maybe she was just being salty because she didn't want to be here.

Don't be stupid, she chided herself. *It wasn't as if you could have stayed in Haven Ridge forever. There's no place to live. No work. No reason to be there in the first place.*

As if to call out the lie in her monologue, her memory supplied not last night's kiss, but the hours before it—walking through town, sitting by the hot springs, talking about things she hadn't had the courage to admit to anyone else. She shook her head angrily, garnering strange looks from a passer-by. A man was not a legitimate reason to move somewhere, at least not one she'd known for two days. She'd already learned that the hard way.

It was the reminder that she needed to get over her foul mood and get on with her work. She spoke with a few business owners. She interviewed visitors who had come for the festival. And even though she knew it wasn't going to be her best work, at least she would have something to turn in to her editor that was not based on hearsay and wishful thinking.

It was the best she could do right now.

It was getting dark by the time she returned to her vehicle and climbed into the front seat with a heavy sigh. She pulled out her phone and checked VacayAway and Better Rentals, but just like the last time she checked, there was no availability within fifty miles of Salida. That meant she was driving to Colorado Springs tonight to get a motel room and write her article. Fine. She was more than ready to leave this stretch of mountain road behind her. She'd give it a fond farewell, use up the last of her money on gas to get back to Washington, and forget this little interlude had ever occurred.

Her eyes were sticky and stinging by the time she pulled into the parking lot of a semi-reputable motel on the west side of Colorado Springs, and she wearily went through the motions of renting the room. Once she unlocked her door with the key card—a step up from the motel in Denver for sure—she rolled her suitcase to the bathroom's tile floor and checked the whole place for signs of bedbugs and flesh-eating fungus. Not that she believed she could actually see something like flesh-eating fungus. When she was convinced that it was indeed clean and would not require her to fumigate herself after a shower, she pulled the flowered bedspread off the hard mattress, propped herself up against the headboard amid a sea of pillows, and got down to work.

And realized one important thing about writing. She didn't love it.

She'd always known that she wasn't a writer, not in the way that professionals were, relishing the crafting of messages in words. As a history student, writing had always been a necessary evil, a way to convey her findings in order to share them with her professors, or later, the world. It was the information about which she was passionate. But as she started to craft an article about a perfectly nice town and a perfectly nice festival, neither of which held any real interest for her, she realized the truth.

This had all just been another way to pretend that she was moving on, that she was someone she wasn't. To convince herself she had been right in giving up her dreams and everything she loved for a guy. For a relationship that hadn't gone anywhere. For a relationship that hadn't been worth it at all.

It was time to stop running. It was time to stop pretending that she was okay, that she was anyone other than who she was. It was time to stop throwing good decisions after bad, trying to justify the one big mistake in her life that had affected everything else. And she knew, as she typed the final line of her article somewhere after two a.m., that this would be the last one she would write.

She opened an app message, and after a moment's thought, began to type.

Dear Bea,

Unfortunately, I wasn't able to find the documentation that you wanted for the Haven Ridge story, so I went ahead and wrote the one on Salida that I promised you. Personally, I think Haven Ridge is the more interesting angle, but I understand if you're not comfortable running it. I'm attaching both articles so you can make your own decision about which one you want to use.

Thank you for your confidence in me these past months. I've enjoyed the opportunity to see this area of the country and visit interesting places. But I am not a writer. I'm a historian, and it's time for me to get back to doing what I do best. So I won't be pursuing any future work with Altitude. I appreciate all you've done for me.

Sincerely,

Mallory Adams

She attached the two documents and pressed *send* before she thought about what she was doing. It hadn't been her dream job, but it was a decent job. It had been income at a time that she really needed it, and it was a distraction at a time that she needed it more. But as long as she had a crutch, a justification to keep ignoring her mistakes and not backtrack to the point when it had all gone wrong for her, she wouldn't be able to move on. Wouldn't be able to find the thing she was really meant to do in this world. She'd remain a nomad, too afraid to find a place to settle.

And if there was one thing that her unexpected stop in Haven Ridge had taught her, it was that everyone—even she—deserved a place to call home.

* * *

He should give up. He knew he should give up. It was too late for him and Mallory, too late for the article about Haven Ridge. Too late for everything.

But even after it became obvious that Mallory had left, Thomas returned to the storage space and began his search anew. The second floor hadn't yielded anything interesting, but he hadn't even looked at the third floor yet. The stairs here were more rickety, just a set of steeply angled stringers with narrow planks for treads. He climbed them carefully and pushed his way into the unlocked third-floor storage room.

If he'd thought the second floor was daunting, it was nothing compared to this smaller, more tightly packed space. Whereas there had been a few haphazard stacks of boxes below, shoved in around furniture, this room was packed floor to ceiling with them, crumbling with age, the tape that held them together yellowing and curling away from the boxes' dusty sides. And from what he could tell, none of them had useful labels. Numbers, yes, but whatever key had been used to catalog their contents was probably long gone.

Thomas pulled the string on the second bare bulb toward the back, pulled out his knife and Sharpies, and got to work.

The process was endless. Thomas started with the stack near the door, taking down each box, looking inside, labeling their contents before he shifted them to a new stack. Most of it was documents, paperwork from the last seventy years, and not organized in a way that would be useful to anyone. At some point, he and his grandmother needed to sift through them carefully to find anything worth keeping—deeds or insurance policies, for example—and throw away the rest. This felt like his grandfather's doing. Only Grandpa Gerald would keep records from sixty years ago from a bank that no longer existed.

And yet the promise of what he might find in here kept him going, even as hours passed and he found nothing more interesting than his mother's report card. Which admittedly was interesting, especially since she had always claimed she was a straight-A student when there was a long period of time where she was lucky to pull Cs. This from a mother who had told him if he wasn't getting As, he wasn't trying hard enough? He grinned and set that stack of papers aside. He'd scan them and email them to his mom in Spain, just to needle her a little.

He lost track of time sifting through boxes, the work taking on its own sort of dreamy rhythm. Until his phone buzzed in his back pocket and he caught the time stamp on the text message from Madeline. 3:30. **Will you be back in the restaurant soon? I need to leave at 4.**

That's right. He was completely shirking his duties at the restaurant, and he'd dumped the responsibility on Madeline. He quickly taped up the box he was looking through, scrawled a description of its contents on the top and sides, and dropped it onto a stack. He'd come back. He had to. Even though it was probably already too late for the article, this had taken on the feel of a quest. It wasn't only about giving Mallory legitimate references for her work. It was about proving to Mallory that everything they'd said about the town was true.

He went back down to the restaurant, washed up in the restroom, and dismissed Madeline, taking his place behind the counter. But after their usual crop of Sunday early-birds came in between four and six, there wasn't much traffic to keep him occupied. His mind wasn't there anyway. When it wasn't on the upstairs storage room, it was on Mallory.

She hadn't said goodbye. True, he supposed his words to her before he'd left her apartment last night had been a pretty emphatic farewell, but he'd meant it as a warning to himself not to derail her plans, not from a desire to never see her again. Had he known that she would leave without a trace, without a single goodbye, he would have . . .

What would he have done? It wasn't as if he was going to kiss her goodbye. He wouldn't be able to convince her to stay, even if he could somehow convince himself it was the right thing to do. And he certainly wasn't going to guilt trip her over how much the town needed that little bit of publicity she could provide.

It was just that now that she was gone, he realized he would miss her.

In those two days, she'd brought light and vibrance back into his life. He couldn't even pinpoint why. It had just been her presence. The way she smiled. Her enthusiasm over small things that he took for granted. The sadness beneath the determination when she told him about her parents and how her aunt hadn't exactly been a soft place to land. Neither of them had had an easy life, and he supposed that someone could argue that he had it worse, losing his wife, but he'd been lucky. He'd had his grandmother and Haven Ridge to come back to. Mallory had nothing. And yet she still went on every day with hope, even when it meant scraping by in a life that wasn't even close to what she had envisioned for herself.

He liked her. He admired her. And now that she was gone, out of his reach forever, he thought that maybe he could have come to love her.

"Great timing as usual," he muttered to himself grimly. "I always come to these realizations too late." Estella had always joked with him that he was the dumbest sensitive man she'd ever met; he could evoke the emotions of a sunset in an abstract painting, but he couldn't recognize his own feelings until it was too late to act on them. Had it not been for Estella's sense of humor and patience—she had been the one to finally ask him out in the end—he might have gone on being single forever. But she was gone and now so was Mallory.

As soon as the clock turned to eight, Thomas flipped the sign, locked the door, and called to Arnold that he was going back up to storage. This time he attacked the boxes like a man possessed, though he quickly found out that speed and passion didn't miraculously make the contents any more interesting.

And then, somewhere around ten thirty, he hit pay dirt.

It was a cardboard box like any other, but when he opened this one, it wasn't bank statements or old report cards or any other useless detritus of a long, average life. Instead, it held three leather-bound photo albums and a small polished wood box.

Thomas dragged the packing box over beneath one of the light bulbs for a better look and wiped his dirty hands on his jeans before he flipped open the cover of the first book. He sucked in his breath.

The photos were old. Not just old in the sense that the others were old, but clearly not modern. The sepia tones had faded over the years, but it was clear as he turned from one page to another that these were from the early days of Haven Ridge. And not just a handful. Dozens.

How did they manage to take so many? he wondered, picturing the old-style box cameras with the drape that went over the photographer's head. He'd always been under the impression that photographs were expensive and only reserved for special occasions, which was why they were so rare.

Or maybe these *were* special occasions, worthy of the cost to record them.

Here was Columbine Street, back in its timber-framed days, where the buildings were spread out with space around them and hitching rails stood in front of most. He didn't recognize any of the buildings, having only known the brick structures that replaced them, but their signs identified their purpose. Bank. Boarding house. Feed store. Laundry.

And then, when he flipped the page, he drew in a breath. The Brick House Cafe.

Or rather, the Strong Supply Depot, the location that would later become the cafe. Even if it weren't for the sign, he'd know it by the oak tree that grew on the corner, just barely visible in the edge of the photo. Even half the size it was now, it already had its distinctive shape, one large branch sheared off near the trunk from a lightning strike. It still bore that scar today, giving it a lopsided look even as it towered at nearly one hundred fifty feet. In this photo, there were three women, clothed in the prairie dresses that he recognized from old movies, their hair worn up. Two of them wore bonnets, but the woman in the middle stared right at the camera, back straight and head bare, a coiled bullwhip hanging from her belt. He held up the book so he could take a closer look at her face and saw the unmistakable resemblance to his grandmother. This had to be Elizabeth Strong.

His stomach flipped over and he carefully peeled away the plastic covering from the page. Too late he realized he shouldn't be handling century-old photographs with dirty bare hands, so he used a fingernail to pry it from the backing and flip it over.

On the back, in old-fashioned writing, the ink blurred and faded from time, he read: *Opening of the Strong Supply Depot, Haven Ridge, Colo, September 1880. Millicent Edwards, Elizabeth Strong, Constance Tolliver.*

Excitement built in his chest. This was it. This was the thing he'd been looking for. Proof that the town had existed when and how his family had always claimed. Photographic proof that not only did Elizabeth establish a mercantile on this very site, but she'd done it herself with the help of other women.

History might not be his thing like it was Mallory's,

but even he knew this was revolutionary. He snapped a photo of the front and back and opened his text messages ... then realized he didn't have Mallory's number. Or her email. Or any way to contact her.

But there was always Google. He opened his browser, searched for her name, and came up with the expected nearly thirteen million hits. The first several were for an actress by the same name, which he immediately dismissed. Then he moved on to the scattering of social media profiles, clicking on each and every one before determining that they weren't his Mallory.

He paused. His Mallory. He didn't have the right to think of her that way, even if he liked the way it sounded.

After twenty minutes of clicking every link and getting nowhere, he finally added a series of search criteria with her name, one by one: *history, writer, Idaho.* She wasn't on the masthead at her magazine, and even when he searched for her name on their website, he got no hits.

Who in this day and age didn't have a digital footprint? If he didn't know any better, he'd think she was a ghost or these last two days had been a figment of his imagination.

He replaced the photo album back in the box and shoved it toward the door, returning his attention to the remaining two dozen that were left. But none of those yielded the same bounty as the one he'd just found; lots of family photos which he would no doubt want to see later, but didn't fit his single-minded search.

When he had gone through every last box, Thomas hoisted the one containing the photos and brought it back to his apartment, where he plopped it on the coffee table. Then he thoroughly washed his hands and returned to the album.

With every photo and every album, his wonder increased. It seemed that Elizabeth had understood the revolutionary nature of what she was doing, because she had documented every step. There were photos of the original timber buildings, and then the brick ones that followed them right before the turn of the century. It was like watching a time lapse of the town; if he created a flip book, he could fan the pages and see it taking shape right before his eyes. There was Elizabeth, as its mayor, cutting a ribbon in front of the granite bank in 1906, her hair coiffed in a Gibson Girl style, her pale ruffled dress the height of fashion. Over time, more and more men appeared in the photos, but it seemed clear that women retained the primary role for a good long while. All the stories about Elizabeth building Haven Ridge as a respite for families and single women and widows seemed to be true. Only it had gone far beyond that as other people needing a safe haven had found their welcome here.

It was an astounding find. It could possibly change everything that historians understood about this town and its impact on this part of Colorado. It was exactly what Mallory had been looking for.

And he had no way of telling her.

CHAPTER SEVENTEEN

MALLORY ENDED UP STAYING in Colorado Springs for another month. It wasn't so much a choice—though the city was large and had everything she could possibly need—but because as soon as she had turned in her articles, she was hit with a wave of inertia. She knew what she had to do to move on, but she couldn't convince herself to do it.

It didn't help that the motel that she'd landed in was actually pretty nice and she struck up a friendship with the woman, Lillian, who worked the day shift in the office. When she'd heard that Mallory was in need of a job, she hired her to work the night shift with no questions and no references. It wasn't a difficult job, and they only got one or two late travelers each night, so most of the time Mallory sat at the desk alone and read book after book checked out from the nearby public library.

It also didn't help that getting answers on whether or not she could resume her degree at the University of Washington had been frustratingly difficult. It seemed that because she'd quit abruptly in the middle of a

semester and not formally transferred out, she was in
some sort of weird administrative limbo. The department secretary sent her to the registrar, who sent her to
transfer admissions, who sent her back to the chair of
the history department, who Mallory knew well but
happened to be in China for the summer and wasn't
responding to emails.

The one thing that she did figure out quickly was
that her grant through the university would not be
available to her and she'd missed the deadline to apply
for federal student aid for the fall semester by about two
weeks. It was enough to make her scream. She finally
had a direction for her life. She was trying to make good
on all her old plans, undo the mistakes that had taken
her so off course. And all she hit were roadblocks.

Until she was walking around Old Colorado City, the
historic district in the west part of town, and passed a
bookshop. Out of curiosity, she wandered inside. After
browsing the shelves for a few minutes and making notes
of books she wanted to check out from the library—her
budget didn't stretch to nonessential purchases at the
moment—she passed the register. And there, right in
front, was a stack of this month's *Altitude Magazine*.

She snapped it up and flipped through to the travel
section. Bea had responded to her email by saying she'd
consider carefully which one she wanted to use—and
generously paid Mallory for both articles—but she
hadn't ever told her what the final decision had been.
Mallory found herself holding her breath as she
scanned the pages. And then she froze.

There it was: *Mountain Haven: the Surprising History of
a Forgotten Colorado Town.*

Immediately, Mallory brought the magazine to the
counter and paid for it, then rushed outside to a bench
where she could sit and read. It was her article all right,

word for word except for a few judicious edits for length, and punctuated with the photos she'd taken on her tour with Thomas. Even the thought of him pierced her heart with a quick, sweet ache, but she shoved it away and turned her attention back to the article. The joy building in her chest was out of proportion to the actual accomplishment; all she could think of was how beautiful and idyllic she had made the town seem. If she were reading this article, she would want to plan a trip there immediately.

And then at the end of the article came a surprising disclaimer.

> Editor's Note: While much of this history cannot be corroborated by primary sources, small-town legends and oral history, however apocryphal, are vibrant and important parts of our local culture. Altitude Magazine makes no warrant as to the veracity of the claims herein and encourages interested parties to do their own research. Or as we do, enjoy the idea that one of our local, forgotten treasures was forged out of necessity and hard work, like all of the American West.

It was a graceful way of saying that they had no idea if her story was true, but they didn't care because it was too good not to share.

Mallory sat back against the bench, savoring the article for a moment. It made no difference to her decision; she still maintained that she was not a writer, she was a historian. But it was closure on a brief chapter of her life. She'd done what she'd set out to do. She'd accomplished everything she could for Haven Ridge, in return for what it had done for her—make her realize the things that she was missing in her life and give her the motivation to pursue them.

Impulsively, she jumped up from the bench and hurried back down the street, then made a quick turn down an intersecting one. Ten minutes later, she arrived at the post office in the historic district, a yellow block building in an imposing style not unlike Haven Ridge's bank. She pulled the door open, stepped into its cool, surprisingly quiet interior, and stepped up to the packaging kiosk, where she slid the magazine into a Priority Mail envelope. Just before she sealed it, she thought better of it and pulled out a pen and the receipt from the bookstore, where she scrawled a note.

Thomas, they went with the article anyway! I hope and pray that this helps Haven Ridge in some way. Thanks for everything. Mallory

She shoved the receipt, writing up, between the first two pages of the article and replaced the magazine in the envelope. With help from the internet, she addressed it to Thomas Rivas at the Brick House Cafe, paid for the postage at the self-serve kiosk, and dropped it through the package drop.

She smiled to herself, even as she felt that slight, insistent ache in her heart. Now she was finally done.

* * *

"Mail for you, Thomas."

Carolyn Calligaris, Haven Ridge's postmaster *and* only mail carrier, dropped a pile of mail on the cafe's counter, then made a swift turn and left the building in a tinkle of bells before Thomas could even thank her. He swept the pile off the counter, noting the usual complement of bills and junk mail before he saw the thick envelope beneath it. It was addressed to him in a feminine hand, no return address. Frowning, he grabbed the tab and ripped it open.

A copy of *Altitude Magazine* lay inside. He clamped down on the sudden surge of hope as he drew it out, fanning through the pages until it opened to an article in the center, marked with a scrap of paper. *Mountain Haven*, it was called. With a huge photo of Haven Ridge's main street.

His heart leaped into his throat as he skimmed the article. How could this be? Mallory had said there was no way they would print the article without corroboration, and he hadn't been able to reach her with the photos. But sure enough, it was all about the town and its interesting history, even if the editor's note at the end implied that it could all be made up.

He took a long deep breath and let it out, hope flooding his body. Maybe it wouldn't make a difference. Maybe they were doomed to dwindle away. But they'd tried. *Mallory* had tried. And it was clear from her writing that she had fallen in love with the place as much as those who had been born here. Somehow, she had captured the warmth and the friendliness despite the fact they were fading away. It made him want to plan a trip, and he already lived here.

And then he noticed what he thought was a scrap of paper was actually a note. From Mallory.

His heart rose at that small communication with her, the look of her looping script, and fell just as quickly as he registered the friendly but distant tone of the note. As if he hadn't kissed her for all he was worth the night before she left. As if he hadn't thought about her every night since then, alternately missing her and hoping that she'd found what she was looking for. That she hadn't been in contact with him because she was too busy planning her fabulous new life in Washington.

He flipped the paper over and saw it was a receipt for the magazine. And not just any receipt, but one from a familiar bookstore in Colorado Springs. Two days ago.

He stared, his heart pulsing in his chest, throbbing in his ears. She was still here. Why was she still here? Why hadn't she gone back to Washington like she'd planned?

Then reality crashed in. If she'd wanted him to get in touch with her, she would have written a return address. This had been a courtesy and nothing more. She clearly didn't want to see him. That single weekend had obviously meant a lot more to him than it had to her.

And yet ... she didn't know about the town. Didn't know that everything she'd written was true. Maybe it made no difference in the grand scheme of things, but didn't she deserve to know? She was a historian after all. She'd been enchanted by the possibilities. And even if the reason she lingered in Colorado had nothing to do with him or Haven Ridge, he couldn't let her leave without telling her they hadn't lied to her or made up stories or been wrapped up in wishful thinking. It was all true.

And maybe if that was all true, maybe Elizabeth Strong's vision was true too. Maybe the magic is real.

He pulled out one of the old-fashioned phone books beneath the counter, opened it to the section he needed, and started to dial.

CHAPTER EIGHTEEN

FOR ALL HER BRAVE TALK about moving on, she was still here.

It had been three days since Mallory had mailed the magazine to Thomas, and however final that action had seemed, it hadn't been enough to spur her to check out of the motel and drive back to the Pacific Northwest. She kept telling herself it was because even if she sorted her university problems, she couldn't start classes until the fall, and the summer weather was better in Colorado than in Washington. But she knew the truth. She didn't want to go back to Seattle without arrangements in place, and there was no way she was going to beg her way back into her aunt's house in Portland, only to sit and stew. So Colorado Springs was as good as any other place. For now.

She arrived at her room from her afternoon walk a few minutes before she was scheduled to go on shift, with just enough time to take a shower, put on a little makeup, and grab her reading material for tonight. One was a surprisingly boring and uneven history of Colorado—with each passing page, she couldn't help but mentally note the missed opportunities within to talk about the role of women and people of color in the state, not to mention the history and culture of the native tribes—and the other a historical romance that somehow managed to feel more accurate and alive than the history book. She had a feeling she knew which one she'd be reading for most of her shift tonight.

Lillian was already packing up when she finally wandered across the parking lot and into the outdated, bare-bones office.

"Hot date?" Mallory quipped, looking over her friend. The fifty-year-old was recently divorced and had been talking about the difficulties of hitting the dating scene at her age. Mallory wanted to commiserate, but she hadn't been brave enough to dip her toes into the waters at twenty-seven.

"Actually," Lillian said loftily, "I do. I met someone at the gym. We're going out to dinner tonight." She looked at Mallory with a knowing look. "Have fun, you, and don't neglect your duties."

Mallory frowned, confounded by the statement, but Lillian was out the door before she could ask for clarification. Maybe she was talking about her reading material? It wasn't like there was much to do—some occasional filing, vacuuming the carpet, straightening up the employee restroom. But mostly, she just read books, watched Netflix on her phone, and tried not to fall asleep until Lillian was back at six to take over.

She was wiping down the counter when movement caught her eye—a vehicle pulling into the parking lot. Just in case it was a guest, she swept her books under the counter and opened the reservation system on the computer. No one was scheduled to come in tonight, which probably meant it was a walk-in. They got far more of those than they got advance reservations. Not a surprise for something called the Sleep Well Inn.

Except as the man climbed out of his vehicle—a familiar vehicle—her heart started pounding in her ears and her breath seized in her lungs. She had to be imagining this. As he moved toward the glass door, a backpack slung over one shoulder, she rubbed her eyes, sure that this was some sort of strange urban mirage. There was no way that he could be here.

And then Thomas was through the door and standing before her, smiling uncertainly. "Hi."

She blinked. "Hi."

"I hope you don't mind me dropping by. Lillian said she'd thought it would be okay."

Lillian. Ohh. Now her comment made more sense. But how ... .why ... ? She shook her head, trying to jolt herself back into some semblance of logic. "What are you doing here?"

"I got the magazine yesterday. Thank you."

"But ... what are you doing *here*?" she repeated. It was a good thing she had given up writing, because apparently she had used up her allotment of coherent sentences.

His cheeks colored above his beard, and her heart squeezed a little. She'd forgotten how endearing that shyness was, the fact that he was a man who actually blushed. He met her eyes, though, and the look in them took her breath away. "I hope you don't mind. I know it's kind of invasive and I don't want you to think I'm a creepy stalker ... "

"I didn't think that until now," she said slowly.

He laughed. "I saw the receipt you used for the note. The bookstore isn't that far from here. So I thought if you were still in Colorado Springs, you might have gotten a room at a motel. And about ... twenty calls later, Lillian confirmed for me that you were indeed a guest."

Lillian again. So she'd kept this under wraps for at least a day, maybe more. "I . . . I don't know what to say. It's nice to see you. It really is. But why did you come here?"

"Oh." He deflated a little, then hoisted his backpack up onto the counter. "I wanted to show you something."

He unzipped the backpack and pulled out a heavy leather-bound photo album, then pushed it across the counter to her. Gingerly, she flipped it open and then sucked in a breath.

They were photos. Old photos, but not the formally posed ones that she was used to from the era. These were the Old West equivalent of selfies, people in groups, in front of buildings, going about their business. And if she wasn't mistaken, it was . . .

"Haven Ridge," she breathed. "You found these?"

"In the storage above the cafe." He reached forward to flip a page and then tapped one with his fingernail. "Do you recognize this one?"

"Strong Supply Depot!" Mallory exclaimed. She looked closer. "Is that Elizabeth Strong?"

"It is. And all the ladies are identified on the back with the date. September 1880."

"That's amazing," she said, flipping through the pages slowly, poring over the photos. "What a treasure. So it's all true? All the stories? Do you know that I tried to verify all the facts with a professor at the university here before I sent in the article, and he told me there was absolutely no documentation on the town? He thought that it was probably founded by someone named Bixby."

"Oh, he's in here too, but he came later. Much later. About the time the bank was built in fact, and he started building what is essentially a castle outside of town. I should have showed it to you, but it's been closed up for so long, frankly I forgot about it."

"This is wonderful." She gave a happy sigh, closed the book, and pushed it across to him. "Thank you for showing it to me."

He stared at her. "But ... I thought you might want to ... "

"Keep it? Of course not. It's your family's legacy. Someone will want to write a book about it someday."

"I know," he said softly. "I was hoping that someone might be you."

She froze, catching the soft look on his face. She'd been afraid to let herself think of this visit as anything but a courtesy, a justification of her work, but the way he was looking at her now had nothing to do with history or family legacy. At least not directly. She swallowed hard. "Why?"

"Because," he said, his voice as soft as his expression, "I miss you. Things haven't been the same since you left. And I'd convinced myself that I was just being sentimental, that I had kind feelings toward you because our two days together made me realize that I needed to let Estella go and move on. But the more time passes, the more I realize it's because of you. Who you are, who you might become. The way that your smile is kind of crooked, and you get so excited about small things, and you see the world around you not just how it is, but how it was and it could be. And because ... " He broke off and took a deep breath. "Because I want to be with you."

Mallory felt like time had slowed down and she was thinking through mud. There was no way he could be saying what she thought he was saying. She'd thought about him all the time since she'd left, but she'd never allowed herself to believe that he might feel the same way. And however much she wanted to say the words, *I want to be with you too,* she couldn't bring herself to say them. Not until she knew the cost.

"How would that work?" she asked quietly, her eyes locked to his.

"I guess that all depends on you." He reached across the counter and took her hand between his own, brushing his fingers gently over her palm, but his eyes never left her face. "I know you want to go back to school. We do have universities here, and with all this information, I suspect you have a really compelling thesis topic. But I understand you might not want to do that, or you can't. So, if you have to go back to Washington, I guess … well, I've always kind of wanted to paint the Pacific Northwest landscape."

"You … you would move?"

His gaze never wavered. "If I have to. I came back to Haven Ridge because I didn't know what else to do. I didn't know what—or who—I wanted. I do now. If that means I have to move again, to see where this goes, then I'm okay with that compromise." He smiled. "I'd rather be with you somewhere else than in Haven Ridge alone."

She couldn't hold back the smile that spread over her lips. "You'd do that. For me. A woman you barely know."

"I have a suspicion that you're worth it."

The moment stretched, and then as if they were of one mind, they leaned over the counter so their lips met. Softly, gently, at first, until the kiss became more urgent and she was stretched over the counter between them, hands in his hair, heart pounding so loud she thought she might be disturbing the guests next door. And then he pulled back slightly, smiling, brushing hair away from her face while he looked into her eyes. "So, what do you think?"

"I think," she said slowly, "that I'd rather be in Haven Ridge with you than anywhere else … even if it does mean a pretty substantial commute back here for school."

He grinned, then hopped up onto the counter and swung over to the other side so he could gather her to him. "So we're going to do this? We're going to give this thing—us—a go?"

She smiled up at him. "Absolutely."

Then they were kissing again, pouring out every bit of their hope and faith and gratitude that the slim chance of their meeting had not been chance after all, that it had been orchestrated by a power outside themselves. And for the first time, Mallory believed a few words as absolute truth.

What Haven Ridge wants, Haven Ridge gets.

WANT MORE HAVEN RIDGE?
THE STORY CONTINUES IN
THE BROKEN HEARTS BAKERY

TURN THE PAGE FOR A PREVIEW

AVAILABLE IN PAPERBACK AND E-BOOK
EVERYWHERE BOOKS ARE SOLD

EXCERPT FROM
THE BROKEN HEARTS BAKERY

HAVEN RIDGE HIGH SCHOOL was exactly as Gemma remembered it. The main school building was still that weird post-modern mixture they'd always made fun of, a sort of Bauhaus style filtered through Colorado Rustic, with lots of black-framed glass and cantilevered roofs. The grounds, which would be in full greenery later in the year, were the yellow-brown of grass that had recently been buried under inches of snow, the trees still bare of their spring buds. The large asphalt parking lot was scattered with a handful of cars—the beaters that the kids drove and the slightly nicer beaters that the teachers drove.

She smiled as she wove up and down the aisles, guessing that since there were no kids lingering outside the front doors, she'd find Taylor hanging in the lot near someone's car.

She was right. She glimpsed Taylor's blue-streaked ponytail and Doc Martens in a clutch of girls standing next to a decrepit Plymouth and pulled into a parking spot a couple of spaces away. Apparently, the great date betrayal had been forgiven, or at least the drama was still unfolding. Taylor waved but didn't rush over to the car, so Gemma hopped out and wandered to her side.

"Hey," she said, when the conversation stopped and all eyes turned toward her. She smiled at the girls, but focused on Taylor. "Are you ready to go?"

"In just a second," she said. The girls giggled.

Gemma frowned, suspicious. "What's going on?"

"Nothing," a pretty blonde said airily, though she still wore a secretive smile. "I'm Layla, by the way." She stuck her hand out.

Surprised, Gemma shook it. "I'm Taylor's aunt, Gemma. Kind of," she added with a smile.

"Yeah, Taylor told us. Cool that you could come out and stay with her for a little while."

The girls started giggling and whispering again, and Layla nudged Taylor in the ribs. Her niece flushed beet red and hissed, "Shut up! You guys are so embarrassing."

Okay, this had to have something to do with a boy. Gemma recognized that I-want-to-sink-into-the-asphalt posture all too well. Curious, she craned her neck to see who they were looking for. An athlete, no doubt, if they were hanging out in the parking lot so late; she'd spent far too much of her high school career waiting for the football team to leave practice.

Finally, she got a glimpse of a boy coming their way, dressed in athletic gear with a duffel bag slung over his shoulder. She'd been right about that part at least. But as he came closer, she realized it wasn't a boy, but unmistakably a man. Not even football players were that well filled out in high school. Gemma stifled her grin with difficulty. Dear, sweet, prickly Taylor had a crush on a teacher.

"Here he comes," one of the girls sing-songed, while another one sighed, "He's so hot. Seriously. Why does he have to be our teacher?"

"Like that makes any difference," Layla said. "We're all still jailbait."

Gemma wasn't sure whether to be amused or horrified, and she was so focused on choosing between the two that she wasn't paying nearly enough attention when the teacher stopped at a muddy truck a few spaces away and waved at them. "Night, girls. See you tomorrow."

The blood drained from Gemma's face, her stomach taking a downward plunge to the pavement. That voice. She'd recognize it anywhere, even roughened and deepened in the fifteen years since she'd heard it last. Her heart instantly skipped a beat, her traitorous body responding to the sound as if she'd been waiting her whole adult life to hear it again.

Automatically, she swiveled on her heel, turning her back to him, and a word slipped out of her mouth that Liv definitely would not approve her using around her stepdaughter.

She couldn't have done anything that would pique the girls' interest more.

Taylor frowned. "Do you know Mr. Osborne?"

Mr. Osborne. Apparently, there were things that Liv had forgotten to mention to her, or maybe purposely omitted. Slowly, Gemma turned back to the girls, but her eyes sailed right over the teens and landed on the man, who was now staring back at her.

Just get in your truck and drive away, she pleaded silently as the blood rushed back to her cheeks in a furious flush.

No such luck. He was coming their way, his eyes fixed on her. Except for Taylor, the girls spread out, making her feel suddenly, terribly exposed.

"I don't believe it," he said when he was finally standing in front of her. "Gemma, is that actually you?"

Gemma had known coming here was a bad idea. A terrible idea. She automatically straightened to her full height, something that usually made her feel powerful given she literally looked down on half her colleagues while wearing heels, but she didn't have heels today and he'd put another couple of inches on his already-tall frame. "Stephen. I had no idea you taught here."

"Yeah," he said slowly, still staring at her with an expression of confused wonder. "I teach English Lit. And I coach the track team, of course. How are you?"

"Good. I'm good." She had no idea where to look, because everywhere her eyes landed, it just reminded her why she'd fallen for him in high school and how very little had changed since then. His hazel eyes were just as beautiful as she remembered, fringed in lashes so long and dark they made every female jealous. His handsome, boyish features had instead become chiseled and rugged, particularly now, shaded by a five-o'clock shadow. And there was no way she could look anywhere else without him thinking she was ogling.

But oh, how she wanted to ogle.

And that alone made her angry. All she should feel when she looked at him was fury. Or maybe indifference. Certainly not stirrings of the old magnetism that had once made her think that he was her true love, that they were meant to be together, as if his betrayal and the ensuing fifteen years had never happened.

But he seemed to be completely oblivious to her inner turmoil, looking her up and down with bland curiosity. "What are you doing here? Last I heard, you were practicing law in California."

"Yeah. I am. I mean, I was. I . . ." Gemma shook her head to stop her babbling. "I'm just in town for the week while Liv's on a business trip."

"Ah, that's nice." His attention flicked to Taylor, who

was watching the whole exchange through narrowed eyes, then back to Gemma. "We should get together for coffee while you're in town, for old times' sake. My number's in the school staff directory." He smiled at the group of girls, who were clustered around them again, not to be left out of the awkwardness. "Don't forget about your sonnets, ladies. I'm expecting some great things from you."

A chorus of "Okay, Mr. Osborne" came from the girls. He smiled at them all once more, lingering on Gemma for just a few seconds longer, then headed back to his truck with a jaunty wave. All the female eyes followed him, including hers.

Layla was the first to speak. "You knew him," she said, almost accusingly. "You have history."

Gemma shook her head to clear her thoughts and focused on Taylor's friends. "We used to date in high school."

This sparked some laughs and nudges. One of the girls, the redhead—Gemma was really going to have to learn names—asked slyly, "Was he as good-looking then as he is now?"

"Honestly?" Gemma leaned around Taylor to catch one last glimpse of Stephen Osborne as he climbed into his car. "Not really." She shrugged, but even as shell-shocked as she felt right now, she couldn't keep a wry smile off her face. "Some things get better with age."

ABOUT THE AUTHOR

Carla Laureano could never decide what she wanted to be when she grew up, so she decided to become a novelist—and she must be kinda okay at it because she's won two RWA RITA® Awards. When she's not writing, she can be found cooking and trying to read through her TBR shelf, which she estimates will be finished in 2054. She currently lives in Denver, Colorado with her husband, two teen sons, and an opinionated cat named Willow.

Made in United States
Troutdale, OR
02/29/2024

18027347R00105